THE ALLY

THE
ALLY

IVÁN REPILA

Epilogue by Aixa de la Cruz

Translated from the Spanish
by Mara Faye Lethem

OTHER PRESS
NEW YORK

Originally published in Spanish as *El aliado* in 2019
by Seix Barral, an imprint of Editorial Planeta, S. A., Barcelona
Copyright © Iván Repila, 2019
Epilogue copyright © Aixa de la Cruz, 2019
Copyright © Editorial Planeta, S. A., 2019

Translation copyright © Mara Faye Lethem, 2022

Production editor: Yvonne E. Cárdenas
Text designer: Jennifer Daddio / Bookmark Design & Media Inc.
This book was set in Hightower and Goodlife
by Alpha Design & Composition of Pittsfield NH

1 3 5 7 9 10 8 6 4 2

Library of Congress Cataloging-in-Publication Data
Names: Repila, Iván, 1978- author. | Cruz, Aixa de la, 1988- writer of
supplementary textual content. | Lethem, Mara, translator.
Title: The ally / Iván Repila ; epilogue by Aixa de la Cruz ; translated from
the Spanish by Mara Faye Lethem.
Other titles: Aliado. English
Description: New York : Other Press, [2022] | Originally published in Spanish as
El aliado in 2019 by Seix Barral, an imprint of Editorial Planeta, S. A., Barcelona.
Identifiers: LCCN 2022020991 (print) | LCCN 2022020992 (ebook) |
ISBN 9781635422542 (paperback) | ISBN 9781635422559 (ebook)
Subjects: LCSH: Feminism—Fiction. | LCGFT: Social problem fiction. | Novels.
Classification: LCC PQ6718.E688 A6313 2022 (print) |
LCC PQ6718.E688 (ebook) | DDC 863/.7—dc23/eng/20220509
LC record available at https://lccn.loc.gov/2022020991
LC ebook record available at https://lccn.loc.gov/2022020992

Publisher's Note
This is a work of fiction. Names, characters, places, and incidents
either are the product of the author's imagination or are used
fictitiously, and any resemblance to actual persons, living or dead,
events, or locales is entirely coincidental.

LISTEN UP: I'LL TELL IT TO YOU SINGING.

—NACHO VEGAS

0

I'M THE MOST feminist guy you'll ever meet.

But sure, I have my contradictions. Right now, for example, my five roommates and I are throwing eggs at a group of naked and semi-naked women demonstrating in front of city hall. The first two flew past the mark, but the next ones make a perfect impact on the face and tits of the women holding up the main sign. I see our eggs flying in slow motion, describing a lovely arc from down to up and up to down, until they break and become sticky snot, natural and devoid of beauty, and I think about David's slingshot and the outline drawn in the air by the stone before it inflamed the flesh and separated the cartilage from Goliath's bone, and I can't help but think how right I am when I say that there's something platonic about violence.

"The one with the waxed pussy is really hot," says Hugo.

I can't say exactly what the reason is for the protest, because I've been attending these kinds of events for too many weeks now and I confuse the plots, and of course my roommates don't know either, so I don't know who or what I'm throwing eggs at. It could be my mother or my girlfriend. Or my sister. One of my grandmothers is dead. The riot police stationed amid the demonstration and the counterdemonstration start getting nervous when three hundred grams of yolk tint a blonde woman's hair orange, but we're protected by the crowd and still have a dozen ovoid grenades in our pockets, so we stick to the plan. "We won't stop until there are none left," we'd said. I'll admit throwing eggs isn't an original idea. Pathetic, even, when compared to other forms of urban guerrilla warfare in vogue at the time, but it's easy for me to convince the team: eggs are cheap, easy to get and to hide; they aren't a serious enough offense to get us in real legal trouble; and, above all, they represent male virility, our balls, our *huevos*. You don't want balls, right? Well, here are ours, I think I said. Have our *huevos*. The guys loved that, especially Donovan, whose addiction to anabolic steroids has turned him into a 260-pound boy obsessed with his genitals. Calling him a boy is a private joke: he's thirty-five years old. But he still lives with his parents.

"The one on the left, with the freckles, is really hot," says Hugo.

The storm of eggs has raised hackles. Some of the women confront the police and a group of men who were chastising them: cover yourself up, you're whores, if I was your brother, where are you going with that body, in my day... The men [insert any verb conjugated in the third-person plural] things. If I've learned anything during these months of continued exposure to the universe of feminist demonstrations, it's that whatever the protestors are demanding, they can always be upbraided for being women. That might sound grotesque, but it works. It works so well that in the face of a seemingly irreproachable demand like "No more violence against women," you can hear retorts like "You must have done something," with no preamble or nuance. Not on social media, of course, where the aggressor is immediately discredited by the social masses who represent the spirit of what's right, but it works on the street, protected amid many dismayed faces, like at a soccer stadium. These kinds of events are attended by men and women of different ages, classes, and ideologies, and it's relatively easy to shout out any sort of insult—"Get back in the kitchen," for example—and shortly after find a friendly face sharing a complicit smile, or a wink. You know the real deal, buddy. That's how they talk. We guys can show plenty of solidarity too.

"That redhead is really hot," says Hugo.

The police have pulled out their nightsticks, and people are starting to run. I look at my buddies and confirm we're out of eggs. Mission accomplished. We've come up with a powerful language of gestures to communicate any incident during the battle, so I wordlessly suggest leaving the crowd and going back to the car, before we get hurt from a shift in the running mob or a billy club randomly dancing through the horde. As I quickly flee the area, where two cops are trying to separate some protestors from an older man who's raising his fist like a teenager, I see that almost all the women are starting to get dressed. They don't seem satisfied, and their expressions give off a tragic sadness, the pure simplicity of defeat. All except one, who looked young, and was still defiantly naked in a corner. She watches us flee in a way that I recognize, and I signal to her so she'll

notice me. When she does, I lower the handkerchief covering my face, blow her a kiss and give
her the middle finger.

"Whore!" I shout at her.

She doesn't know it yet, but she is about to take
the next step.

PART

ONE

1

MY YELLING "WHORE" at some stranger who's defending her rights all started when I first met Najwa at a Siri Hustvedt lecture. Picture the room: packed with people, mostly women, mostly young women. I don't understand a lot of what's said, partly because neurobiology is not my field and partly because I haven't read any of her books, but I have to admit that the subjects put forth by Paul Auster's wife—as most media outlets refer to her—are interesting, or at least pique my curiosity. The question segment at the end is grotesque, as often happens with such things: people (women) trying to show they know as much or more than the lecturer; people (women) taking advantage of the situation to explain their unresolved personal dramas; people (women) thanking Siri for existing. It seems like an African ceremonial ritual celebrating the arrival of the rainy season. Or the exact opposite: a group of illustrious American citizens shooting at a hurricane to scare it off. Not a single man asks a question, but they don't shoot either. Of course, I don't ask anything. Najwa is the only person (woman) who, during the round of questions, asks Siri about her contradictions and pushes her up against the ropes. Maybe I'm exaggerating. She asks a couple of intelligent, complex questions, without putting on professorial airs. It's fair to point out that Najwa completely looks the part of a highly qualified young woman: in other words, she's wearing glasses. When the event ends and the audience members go up to the stage so that Mrs. Paul Auster will sign books for them, I notice the girl in glasses heading to the exit, and I cut her off so I can talk to her. That's what we men do.

"I liked your questions," I tell her.

She looks at me with scorn in her eyes.

"I'm serious," I insist. "I'm not trying to hit on you. I didn't understand much of anything in the lecture, but I understood your questions."

"You haven't read her books, have you?"

"No. I don't think I could get past the foreword. Do you know if there's a version for kids?"

"I have to go."

"OK. But recommend a book for me. Sorry. That's it and I'll leave you alone."

"What kind of a book?"

"On feminism. So I can start to understand. I'll leave the neurobiology for later."

"Just google 'feminism.'"

"I've done that. Even the Wikipedia entry seems too hard for me. Is there something like *Foucault for Dummies*, but about this?"

It was the first time I saw her smile. I make a mental note: "Foucault."

"Do you have somewhere to write it down?" she asks me.

I pull out my cell phone and open the Notes app. She dictates *Men Explain Things to Me*, by Rebecca Solnit, and *Sexual Politics*, by Kate Millett. Despite having studied literature, I don't know who they are.

"Thank you," I say in parting.

She nods with a half smile, the other side of her mouth obviously weary of me, and she leaves.

I go straight to the library, which closes at ten, to get the books she'd recommended. At the lending desk a woman helps me, and I start feeling a little anxious from what I can only define as excessive environmental estrogens, like the toxic cloud you see in photographs of Mexico City. Siri, her fans, Najwa, the librarian. The feeling is reinforced when my mother calls and details *her* mother's latest offense. It seems my one living grandmother was pissed off because her daughter doesn't visit as often as she should, and meanwhile the librarian comes over with an extraordinary smile and the books. And as I'm leaving I pretend to be listening to my mother and wonder why women smile so much: Why do they smile when it's almost ten at night and they're still working, why do they smile when someone chases after them after a lecture, why do they smile when someone says something impertinent to them in front of other people, I don't know, why do they maintain that unabashed inertia? I try to imagine myself smiling like that, all the time, being complacent with stoic composure, and I don't feel comfortable. I mean: I couldn't do it. All that smiling confuses me, and in a synecdoche that would delight a psychoanalyst, I imagine that their vaginas are also always smiling, happy faces, in what seems to be an exhausting muscular effort worthy of an elite gymnast, and it seems stupid. Women's candid nature is one of their weak points.

When I get home I remember why I went to the lecture.

Subject A: thirtysomething. I don't know what he does for work. I've been living with him for nine months. His favorite tags are "Gangbang" and "Facefucking." He has an iPhone 7 Plus. On the weekends he races his bike up in the mountains. He hardly drinks alcohol, but he likes marijuana. He never puts down the toilet seat.

Subject B: twentysomething. I don't know what his job is. I've been living with him for six months. His favorite tags are "Anal pain" and "Anal pain teen." He has a Chinese phone with a great camera. He goes out every night. He's generous with alcohol and food, but not cocaine. He never cleans up his hair in the shower.

At first it was fun. Three guys on a sofa talking about life, sex, and politics. I don't talk to them about my work, because it's not like I have much to say. Cruel jokes are followed by even crueler ones. We subjected every woman on television to an exhaustive analysis of their female attributes. You're either a tits man or an ass man. We would tell each other things. Like about the first time I heard the word *shrimp* to refer to an ugly girl, from the mouth of a literature professor, at the age of thirteen: "You throw away the head, but you eat the body." All the students seemed to find it hilarious. For my fifteenth birthday, my first girlfriend let me touch her tits. I thought I saw her crying, and I remember thinking that I'd squeezed too hard. I was telling my best friend about it five minutes later, after masturbating. The first time I got a blow job, at eighteen, I couldn't get it up, because of the impact of seeing myself in a situation I'd only seen on a screen before. I told the girl that maybe we could kiss first. She said why, when that was what guys liked. Those kinds of things.

We shared photos of our single female friends. We would spell out the names of porn actresses. We put a "Do not disturb" sign on the door to our room when we had a guest. We would send each other porn videos. We had a typical healthy relationship between adult men.

My inner ally started to writhe when Subject A sent us a video he'd directed himself. It was clearly shot without the consent of the protagonist: the camera was placed in one corner of the room, in a pile of clothes, with little light, and the woman never looks directly into the lens. He does: at time stamp 12:24 he puts her on all fours, with her ass toward the viewer, and before proceeding he turns, winks an eye, and lifts his right thumb to signal his victory. Then he smacks her left butt cheek and she sighs like a happy cat. The entire video lasts 16:45 minutes, HD quality.

That bothered me, and I told him so. At first I tried to seem moderate, reasonable, a good roommate who gets that he has his vices, but also his virtues.

"Don't worry about it," he said.

I argued that taping it was a betrayal of that woman's trust, but sending it to us was probably a crime.

"I can't even remember her name, so I'm not worried about betraying her trust. And it's not a crime if the police don't find out," he said.

I argued that he wouldn't like it if someone did that to his sister. I have a sister. I argued that these things can go viral and end up on the Internet.

"What the fuck is your problem?" he said to me.

The discussion changed tone. Subject B took Subject A's side and I lost my shit. When they knocked down all my explanations—if you consider wielding the counterargument "Are you sure you like ladies?" reasonable in a debate—I got aggressive.

"You guys are bastards," began my speech.

Et cetera. From that day on we didn't say a word to each other when we happened to be in the living room or the kitchen at the same time, and obviously they stopped including me in their house gatherings. I didn't care: I had a solid idea in my head about what was right and what was wrong, and a couple of irresponsible dudes weren't going to force me to reassess that. I wouldn't like a casual lover of mine to videotape us in bed and show it to all her friends, for them to see how I move, what I say, how my face changes at the last minute, how much I pant. For them to see the size of my genitals. For them to watch me in slow motion. For them to add sarcastic subtitles. I can't breathe, just thinking about it.

Luckily, women aren't like us.

As the weeks passed and the small domestic disputes started piling up (over washing the dishes, cleaning the bathroom, paying the Internet and electricity bills on time), the latent tension gradually turned into a grudge, and the grudge into rage, so instead of calling each other by our names, we used friendly, everyday nouns in the vocative.

"Hey, you, clown."

"Leave me alone, idiot."

"Pay what you owe, jerk."

I never took those insults seriously. Until two months ago, when I found them in the living room, in front of the TV, commenting on a soccer match. When I passed by, ignoring them as elegantly as possible, Subject B said: "Look at the feminist, running scared."

And when they saw my face, they knew they'd hit the right nerve, the one that goes from my scrotum directly to my brain, and since then they have only referred to me as "the feminist." I'll admit it's surprising, because they take an adjective I've always interpreted as positive and use it pejoratively. I can't say I find it flattering, though. In fact, deep down, for some reason, it really bugs me.

Feminist, my ass, I think. The thought just comes out spontaneously.

But as I think it I see my sister and my mother, and I force myself to remember that, as far as I know, feminism is about equality between men and women, right? Who could criticize that intent? And yet there's something in the word *feminist* that I don't like, that insults my virility, like when you're a boy and get called "girl" because of the color of some rain boots or some jacket lining, and then I realize that's inconsistent and I sleep badly, with terrible, frightening dreams that affect my performance the next day. Although at my job, nobody cares about my performance.

My recurring nightmare is that I wake up transformed into a woman.

So that's why I went to Siri's lecture today. Because I want to find out where this paradox, this absurd dialectic within myself, comes from. Maybe by immersing myself in that universe in a controlled way, I'll discover that I have no reason to feel uncomfortable. Or maybe I'll learn that I should be afraid, because one should fear a monster.

"Good night, feminist," says Subject A.

I don't talk to my roommates anymore. The last thing I announced to them, before ending our relationship through a text message, is that they shouldn't worry. That I had erased the video, but I would never turn them in to the police. That I'm not a traitor.

Feminist, my ass, I think.

2

I RUN INTO NAJWA a month later, at a roundtable discussion on "New Challenges in Feminism." In general, people are bad at choosing titles, and that must be why there were less than twenty people in attendance. Najwa doesn't recognize me. There is only one other man in the room. At the podium, a woman with short, graying hair meticulously reviews the various situations women are up against today around the world: the refusal of the right to asylum because they aren't recognized as a minority, forced breeding farms in Thailand, arrests for having an accident while pregnant, the salary gap, human trafficking, discrimination, humiliations on television, objectification, hypersexualizing. I'm incapable of following the thread. She supports her words with images, statistics, photographs, video clips, diagrams.

Eventually, by accumulation, everything she says seems like a joke, a comedienne's monologue. I want to laugh and clap, or vice versa. I consider telling a sexist joke during the questions, something discreet, to see how she'd react: "What do you call a woman with PMS and ESP? A bitch who thinks she knows everything." They say being able to laugh at yourself is a sign of maturity. When the event is over I see Najwa leaving, and I run over to her. I have a bad feeling of déjà vu, but I don't try to analyze it.

"I read those books," I tell her.

She looks at me disdainfully.

"What books?"

"The ones you recommended. At the talk by Siri. Solnit and Millett."

Now she places me.

"Oh, yeah. I remember. What'd you think?"

"Well. Solnit is easier, more current, obviously. Even *I* knew some of the things she was talking about. That was a good recommendation for someone at my level. But Millett...Millett's a whole nother can of worms; it starts off good, taking on Henry Miller and all that, but then it gets a bit dry. And the book is long. It kind of dragged."

"Is that so?"

"I think I do that mansplaining thing too. Especially with my mother. Now I know why she gets so pissed off."

"Well that's lucky. I don't know what my mother's problem is."

"It must be that you don't call her often enough. Sorry—you see? I'm doing it again."

I hear a sort of muffled laugh, and I feel like I'm making progress. I walk with her to the stairs. I keep talking.

"Do you think that men can be feminists?"

"Do you think *you* can be a feminist?"

"I don't know, that's why I'm asking."

"What do you want to be a feminist for? To lecture your mother?"

We laugh. My liver hurts, but we're laughing.

"In any case, I'm not sure I understand what Millett's saying."

"About what?"

"About everything being a cultural construction. About there being no real essential differences between men and women. Apart from the obvious, like motherhood, I mean."

She looks at me like a boxer about to explain to a weaker rival who the champion is and why that sometimes has to be made abundantly clear.

"And you think there are?"

"Well, besides periods and that stuff..."

"Come on. Show no fear. Tell me what they are."

I think about smiling vaginas.

"Let's see. In general, you're more friendly. Less violent. More communicative. More discreet. Less noisy."

What I keep to myself: I can't imagine you recording a porn video starring me without my consent, and then sending it to all your friends.

"Uh-huh. And we're naturally inclined toward caretaking, right? And avoiding confrontation. And when you say *communicative*, you really mean *talkative*."

"There are exceptions, of course."

I don't want to say the word *blabbermouth*. I don't want to think the word *blabbermouth*.

"What do you do for a living?" she asks me.

"I'm a journalist. A bad one. I could easily be replaced by a... What about you?"

"I'm working on my thesis. But, on the weekends, I wrestle."

I laugh. She doesn't.

"You don't believe me?"

I don't answer.

"You think because I'm a woman I can't enjoy giving a good beatdown?"

"I didn't say that. But I thought..."

She stops me. She pulls out her phone. Searches through the photos. She shows me a photograph:

it's her wearing some bizarre outfit in a gym. She's got on a cape and colorful boots.

"Wow," I say.

"You have a lot of preconceived ideas you need to work on."

"I can see that. What's your thesis on?"

"Double agents in World War II. But not the men. Enough's already been written about the famous Joan Pujol."

I've never heard of Joan Pujol, but I don't dispute the "famous" label. I'll look him up later on Wikipedia. We keep talking as we walk out onto the street, and then a little longer, standing by the doorway. I notice a pattern: if I don't ask personal questions, the conversation flows; if I do, it stalls. I sense she knows that I know. OK: let's play with subtext. I decide to keep talking until I overcome her resistance just by wearing her out, asking her stuff until she's so thirsty that she needs a beer. I query her on every subject mentioned in the books: postfeminism, virile fallacies, positive discrimination, quotas. One after the other. I confess my doubts to her and I tell her the truth: it seems like a labyrinth. She seems to like my sincerity. She thinks about it. My throat is burning. I see a man sitting comfortably on a wicker chair a few meters away, at an outside bar table, his moustache white

with foam from the first sip, and I salivate. I calculate my chances at 50/50.

"Do you want to have a beer?" I ask.

She accepts, and when we sit down, she takes off
her glasses.

That's a metaphor. But I don't understand it, at
least not right then, because it has to do with me.

3

I DON'T USUALLY have lunch with my parents, much less with the rest of the family. But sporadically they'll organize some sort of telephone tag around a cousin's birthday, and it's impossible to ignore their calls. Like all lobbies, they use blackmail, mostly emotional, to get returns: victimhood, depression, impending death, illness, nostalgia. We aren't allowed to talk about politics, or practically any subject that could spark ideological controversies, so mostly all the talk is trivial philosophy, like the chitchat in elevators. The less of yourself you put into a conversational gambit, the better. Blood kinship: a cognitive repression required to maintain harmony in the epicenter of our basic despair. Too long for a T-shirt. Of course, the presence of young people considerably facilitates the small talk: to the young men, "Do you have a girlfriend?"; to the girls, "Do you have a boyfriend?" Homosexuality is not considered, even in the hypothetical, which says quite a bit about our family. Perhaps the en masse family reunions of the 21st century oblige us to up the ante on the psychoanalytic mandate: it's no longer enough to kill your father: now you have to kill your uncles too.

Like all social groups, we have our dynamics.

For example: the women and children set and clear the table. The adult men don't even attempt to lift a finger. If I do, a woman's voice orders me to sit back down, that there's no need. If one of the women is somehow slightly incapacitated, like with sciatica, for example, she herself will rebel against her handicap and do twice as much as the others. It's a matter of pride. If it's a man who's injured, he gets exclusive treatment: the best cuts of meat, a separate reserve of hors d'oeuvres, a wineglass always full.

For example: the men choose the content of the conversations. The women add their opinions, of course, but they're rarely proactive. If a woman introduces a new subject to the table, the usual dynamic consists of the other women paying attention for a set amount of time, either out of true interest or simple condescension, while the men talk about something else. In any case, the magnetism of that second conversation ends up rendering the first invisible and eventually neutralizing it.

For example: after dessert, when the drinks arrive, the men gather with the men and the women with the women.

Then things get interesting.

Phrase of the day: "Feminists are closeted lesbians."

I don't know why I opened my mouth. Maybe it was the wine. Maybe because I've spent the last two months attending lectures and conferences on feminism, and today I started to appreciate the hidden mechanisms that guide these reunions. Maybe because I wanted to draw attention to myself. But I couldn't help it, and I think that has its origins in my childhood. Or not exactly my childhood, but rather in me at age thirty-five looking back at my childhood from the perspective of my adult self.

Location: living room, after lunch, day.

Characters: my father, my three uncles, fourteen-year-old me, eighteen-year-old me, twenty-four-year-old me.

Scene: the dialogues are interchangeable.

"Don't ever get married, kid."

"You can say that again. If you want to keep fucking, don't get married."

"Women only like sex when they're your girl-friend. After that it's all over."

"They always have a headache."

"Or not even that. Some ache somewhere."

"You can try it once every few months."

"But they get mad."

"They're mad when they do it too."

"They don't like to drink either."

"Coffee. They like coffee."

"And forget about any weird stuff."

"Totally. Missionary and make it quick."

"Don't ever get married, kid."

End of scene.

With those formative precedents, my education is an accumulation of reproaches, jokes, and power games, thanks to which I became an adult able to integrate with most of my peers without drawing too much attention to myself. It's like legalese, but applied to gender: you only understand it if you're part of that group. In this and other families, as a rule, until thirteen or fourteen a boy will remain in the women's circles, and they teach him manners, behavioral norms, what he can and cannot say, and art appreciation; from that age on, the boy stops being a child and is allowed to participate in the men's conversations. They gradually introduce him into professional sports analysis, the search for a relatively economically viable career path, and the complex territory of the battle of the sexes. The use of the word *battle* is not gratuitous. I think my family is typical. We repeat patterns we've inherited from previous generations, patterns that have proved useful for coexistence, and the rule dictates that we will repeat them in the future, if we want to avoid problems. This includes anomalies of all sorts, like that you can drink till you black out or drive in a state just prior to alcoholic coma, but one line of coke is considered a good reason to send somebody to rehab. When I was little they used to warn me about some "druggy cousin." I wonder what they caught that poor cousin doing. Sometime I would like to force a gram of coke into the nostrils of my elders, just to be able to understand their slurred babble after the fourth round of eau-de-vie. Straight from my digit to their noses, like a finger gun aimed right at their nostrils.

"Oh, how disagreeable! I'm so disappointed!" whines one of my aunts.

As I said, I don't know why I ever opened my mouth.

But my uncle and my father made the mistake of returning to their mystical chanting, the Mantra of the Men with No Hole to Stick It Into, and instead of nodding like everybody else and agreeing, I decided to take their colloquium to a higher level—how can I put it, to invoke the excellence of their educations and elevate the brothel repartee to the category of an intellectual debate. A rookie mistake:

you can't question a man's cosmovision without offending the deepest recesses of his identity. I note it for the next time, although I highly doubt they'll invite me again.

Then I see myself, with my most cavalier smile, trying to explain to all those men I grew up with that no, that I don't think they're right, that women like sex as much as we do, that I'm old enough now and I can't complain, that I know of what I speak, and somehow that sets off a crude, bloody fight, splattered with insults and clichés.

"A journalist shouldn't try to lecture us on biology," they say.

Because one of my uncles is a biologist, of course, and my brothers-in-law worship him with the devotion of a supreme engineer of reality, a pagan god, and his knowledge is like the cross and the nails and the crown of thorns: indisputable. The arsenal of pseudoscientific comments he employs to explain the differences between men and women is devastatingly academic, but it hides a tacit defense of old privileges that I can only take as a comic monologue: women release one egg a month, so they don't need to look for sex all the time, but rather be clever and precise in order to find the partner worthy of inseminating that ovum. I serve myself another glass of wine and I bow to him. I'm anesthetized. The pedagogue continues: that's why men are less faithful than women; when you aren't sure that a child is yours, meaning genetically yours, you need to inseminate the greatest number of women as possible. It's just nature. Shooting wildly, without aiming. To ensure that at least one partridge will fall into the basket. I reach a point of no return. I assume that they've all cheated at some point, and I ask them if they think their wives have. That sets off Hiroshima, the cloud billowing.

And just then, while they are overwhelming me with years of behavioral analysis based on their life experience, while they explain the enormous urological differences between men and women, while they use my mother and my aunts as examples to support their theses on human parasexual and inframastubatory habits, and while my mother and aunts remain silent in a corner, as if this had nothing to do with them, and while I—not even knowing what I'm talking about—blend the ideas of Millett, who waves at me from the seventies and tells me we should introduce our families, with various articles by Solnit. The mix is so disastrous that Najwa would be embarrassed, and while I ask them—my fist in the air—when was the last time they ate pussy, or if they even remember how, or if they've ever tried it, and while they seem lost in some grade-school mathematical operation, counting on their fingers, then, in that

moment, in that very moment, I see the opening.
And I shoot:

"Feminism says that—"

Everything that comes after that is a waste of
breath. Which is really a shame, because seeing
how the pillars of my emotional education crum-
ble and all these prudent, sensible family men drop
the administrative mask of responsibility and show
their monstrous Jack the Ripper ways, is pretty
amusing. I feel bad for my aunt.

"Oh, how disagreeable!"

The first thing I hear is that all feminists are
closeted lesbians. The parade of atrocities continues: feminists need to get laid more, feminists never
worked a day in their lives, feminists should go to
college, feminists spend too much time in college,
feminists don't know how to drive, feminists are
so ugly that they can't find a good cock, feminists
need a war, feminists should wax more, feminists
only hang out with other feminists, feminists don't
eat meat.

I argue for the pleasure of laughing at them, although I suspect that's not very ethical behavior.

They ask me to leave. I've soured the atmosphere. I obey.

As I'm leaving I realize that, on a theoretical
level, I didn't make the grade. What the fuck do I
know about what feminism says? I got carried away,

I went with my guts instead of with my head, and fell into textbook discursive sexism: when I don't know what I'm talking about, I pretend I know it all. Not only did I affirm their positions, but I revealed myself as an immature, superficial teenager who's divorced from reality. Maybe it's a good time to ask them for money, like I used to do when I was a kid. I'm sure I could have done better, avoiding direct provocations, not banging my fist on the table, not raising my voice, keeping my calm.

But boys will be boys.

I don't know how to argue without slamming at least one door.

4

I START OBSESSING with small, uncomfortable, everyday situations. I get on the bus and take a seat. Two stops later, an older woman gets on and looks around to find there's nowhere to sit. She remains standing. I wait to see if anyone reacts, and no, nobody bats an eyelash. People are looking at their phones or out the window. It's cloudy. Clouds are always entertaining. I wonder if I should offer her my seat, but I hesitate. If I do, will she think I'm saying she's too old? That I see her as tired, or lame, or needy? I can feel my cheeks sweating, just like when I eat spicy food. I steel myself, and looking into her eyes, I feign giving her my seat. It's a quick, involuntary gesture. She shakes her head.

"I'm fine," she says.

"I don't mind," I tell her.

"I said no."

I sink down into the seat and lower my head. I don't lift it again. I don't know if I've offended her by making her feel weak, if I offended her with excessive, unnecessary, old-fashioned courtesy, if I offended her by making it all about me, or if, actually, she's thrilled I offered. The bus fills up, and I get off three stops earlier than I want to. I'm angry because I don't like feeling insecure, I'm not used to it. I decide never to sit down again.

Spoiler: today I'll end up hitting someone.

As a consolation—because hitting someone is always unpleasant—I decide to get together with my friends.

And my friends are awesome. Although, truth be told, we have increasingly less in common, except for a shared past of alcohol and drugs and never-ending juvenile anecdotes that always keep our get-togethers lighthearted. That time we did such and such. We raise our glasses to the friend we lost along the way. That bachelor party when the future groom kicked the stripper out of the hotel room. Two of my buddies have kids, a house, and a car. Serious professions. The other one is from outer space: no girlfriend, no stable job, no fixed address. The classic nomadic partying surfer dude, who alternates half a gram of hash a day with energy drinks and seitan burgers. We don't look alike.

And our bank accounts don't look alike either. I'm the only one who still lives the way we did when we were in our twenties, and they all tease me about it, which I accept with the serenity of a psychiatric patient on antidepressants. They never ask me about my work, because it bores them. It bores me too. I have savings: maybe I should take a long leave of absence from the office and stop making a jackass of myself for eight hours a day. I jot that down in my mental notebook.

"I met someone," I tell them.

Uproar. A brief interlude about tits, dicks, farm animals, and contraceptive methods. I speak in short sentences, which is a professional bias: I like headlines, lists, inventories; I like to put ideas in order, organize them by color, highlight the news. Their attitude puts me at ease: I know that if I confessed to a murder, they'd joke around for a while before giving me a hand with the shovels and the chain saw. I continue.

"It's quite new. I mean, we haven't been fucking for long. But I like her. And I'm learning a lot."

The word *learning* winds them up, because they've already learned everything that life has to teach them. If you don't know something by the time you're forty, they say, you'll never know it. The rounds come fast and furious. After several bottles of wine we paused to taste a range of herb liquors, which turned my stomach, and now we're slipping into the somnolence of cocktails. I feel my tongue getting thicker but I'm not the only one having trouble pronouncing my *r*'s. Once, in a similar blood alcohol situation, one of my friends broke up a poetry slam with a death threat to the performer; nothing too serious, except he was at the slam with a poetess friend, and basically, he made her look like a fool in front of her whole scene. The typical night that gets way out of hand.

"About what it's like to be a woman in the world, mostly," I continue.

I don't dare to speak the word that starts with an F. It's not the time or the place for a deep discussion, and the truth is that by this hour of the night I don't really care about anything: not feminism, not the patriarchy, not privileges. We're laughing it up, and everything is fair game. I invoke the circus clown inside me. But we're educated and politically active, and always up-to-date on the sensationalistic headlines; we comment on current events as if we were professional tastemakers, deliberating everything with vague solemnity. The way married men avoid talking about their sex lives, while battering us single guys with questions.

"Have you heard about the president's press conference?"

"Does this chick like to take it up the ass?"

I figure my coupled friends omit their venereal details out of respect for privacy, given that I also know their wives. They're liberal, and feminist without going to any extremes, obviously. They're 21st-century guys, married and with daughters. Genital mutilation is barbaric. Women have a right to abortions. Domestic violence is a scourge on society. Both genders are, basically, equal. It's easy to agree with them.

When the last bar closes its doors, we weigh whether we should go hole up in an after-hours joint, or disband. We discuss the pros and cons and check how much cash we have left, because we're far from any ATM. We decide for the second option. Tomorrow a new amusement park is opening up, and it's best to get there right when it opens, before it's too crowded.

On the way home, still together, on a major thoroughfare: a scene.

A man and a woman are arguing on the sidewalk across the street. We watch them. Something inside of us tenses up. And when the man raises his hand and gives the woman some sort of awkward smack, almost a swat through the air, really, I start running, cross the road without looking for cars, and I slam, literally slam, into the guy. I don't have the slightest idea why I did it. My friends run after me. I didn't hit him. I simply used the momentum of my running to slam my left shoulder into his spine, sending the man, who was visibly drunk, flying forward several meters, without even knowing where the impact had come from. He did a corkscrew flip through the air and landed against the ground with all his weight, which was more than two hundred pounds, like a sandbag. My friends arrive. The woman is screaming, insulting the guy. I think we've sobered up all of a sudden.

"You can't do that," one of my friends says to the man.

The guy mutters something. We help him up while we deliver some sort of thesis on civic conduct and respect for women and drinking too much. We stink of gin, but we're four guys and no one's going to argue with us. The woman approaches him and starts to beat him. The guy covers his face while she punches and kicks him, scratching his face and pulling on his shirt. The guy looks like a scarecrow being abused by a gang of parrots. She is so aggressive that we end up surrounding the guy to protect him from her, and we ask the woman to leave, to go home. That we'll take care of it. Of course, who else.

When the guy recovers his ability to stand and speak, bleeding from his nose and with his shirt torn, he tells us his side of the story. That she is very jealous. That she doesn't let him drink, or go out. That it's true he drank too much beer tonight, but he got together with his cousin, and you know how cousins are. That she hits him regularly. That he was just defending himself, that he's sorry, but there was nothing else he could do. That he feels ashamed when she humiliates him in public. What are his buddies going to think?

One of my friends highlights the question of race: he's a "Machu Picchu," a spic, from South America. They have a different culture.

I'm starting to feel dizzy.

Finally, I don't know how, we end up apologizing to the guy and giving him a hug. Especially me, because I feel guilty about the shove. He tells us he's afraid to go home, that he knows he'll really be in for it. We tell him not to worry, that he'll be fine, and we watch him leave, swerving in S shapes. We're perplexed.

"And then you hear people saying that men are never on the receiving end," smiles one of my friends.

Before I can open my mouth, one of my other friends does.

"Dude, that's different. This case is an exception."

"Yeah, sure. But the domestic violence law protects women from men, not the other way around. And we all know there are a lot of false reports."

"A lot?" I ask.

"Yes. A lot. Or a fair amount. Women take advantage of the law to scare the shit out of their husbands. Look it up, I swear. Shit, I know a few cases. Women can get away with whatever they want."

"Statistics say that false reports represent 0.1 percent of all cases," I respond, without really knowing the stats.

"That's because the men don't dare to report it. Didn't you see that guy? He was embarrassed to talk to us! Would you go to the cops if your wife beat you up?"

One of my friends imitates the cliché of a girl punching, with his wrist bent, weakly. I don't want to laugh, but I have to admit it's pretty funny.

"So, you think there shouldn't be a domestic violence law?" I insist.

"I don't know. If we're all equal under the law, a woman hitting a man should be the same as a man hitting a woman, right?"

No one says anything. I want to say something, but I don't know what: my mind is like someone with Parkinson's trying to do origami.

"That law isn't feminist, because feminism demands equality," he adds.

I'm too drunk to respond. I know that I could use something I've heard over the last few months to attenuate his argument, but my head is waterlogged.

"That woman could kill him tonight," says another one of my friends.

We consider calling the police. I stay to one corner of the conversation, distant, looking in a different direction. I hear them fantasizing about the various ways that guy could die in the next few hours: scissors to the throat, a blunt blow to the head, a knife stab in the inner thigh. They come to an apathetic, slacker consensus: he'll be fine, she won't do anything to him, it's just a passionate relationship, it's between them. They accuse me of being a reckless bully, of looking for trouble. They laugh at me, and at the guy, and at the woman.

They're from a different culture, they have other codes of behavior, I hear. And then jokes. We are very amusing when under the effects of alcohol.

When I get home, alone, none of it is funny at all.

5

NAJWA AND I talk a lot.

Not all the time, of course. Sometimes we sleep. But we like to talk, and sex gives me energy.

The first time we slept together wasn't premeditated, it just happened. We had been drinking, more than usual for a Wednesday, and we were joking around in a bar. A man came over to chat with us, and at some point he asked us if we were a couple. I don't know who took the initiative, but there was a discreet kiss, amid giggles, performed by bad actors in the first rehearsal of a play that we found amusing. We enjoy the theater. We kept talking to that guy for a while, like an established, solid couple, and when he left us alone we tried the kiss again, this time without an audience, in earnest. We liked it again. I told her that I would never bring her home to my place. So we went to hers. And from that night on, we started to see each other almost every day.

Najwa asks me simple questions in order to explain complex problems.

"Do you believe in 'happily ever after'?"

I bite her shoulder hard, because the question makes me peckish.

I tell her I find romantic love corny, but not impossible. I mention seductive poets, bouquets of flowers, soldiers returning home after a long time at war. I speak of chivalry, of princes and princesses in fairy tales, of the happiness pact. I list Meg Ryan films and Rocío Jurado songs. She is silent, just observing me. When I finish, it's her turn.

"If a woman earns as much or more than a man, and has freedom of movement, and the same possibilities of becoming a CEO or president, but the most she aspires to is finding her Prince Charming, then she's still an empty woman waiting for a man to fill her up."

Stupidity and semantics team up against me and win: "Do you want me to fill you up? Right now?"

She's patient with me.

She talks about women as objects instead of subjects: the muse, the lady who waits, the stoic wife. She talks about the woman with no initiative, always at the expense of a man's decision, who needs to be saved or rescued; of the woman who only feels complete if she finds true love and marries and has children. Of woman as the ultimate depository of the desires of a man, who will finally conquer her with his courage and intelligence. Woman, therefore, as something to be occupied, like land, like the enemy's castle. A trophy. Property. A uterus. She gives me harsher examples of how romantic love has manipulated relationships and tipped the scales toward abuse: if he's jealous it's because he loves you; if he hits you it's because he loves you; you belong to me or to no one; don't wear those clothes outside; you're nothing without me.

I am listening to her, but while I do I look at her ass. She has a perfect ass, or perfect for my tastes: small and hard. She realizes. She raises her eyebrows, but doesn't criticize me.

"You're exaggerating," I say, trying to follow the conversation without noticing that I'm employing the exact same dynamic I used with my family: eagerly trying to get a word in.

I dispute a few details with her. I tell her that times have changed, that couples aren't the same as before, that now women can vote and go to university and have careers and that housework is shared, that there's a very strong social awareness about abuse, that we aren't soldiers or heroes or poets anymore. I remind her of the Beijing conference of '95, with forty thousand "sisters" in front of the cameras. I try to get her to see the world as filled with possibilities as I see it.

"Yeah, right. That's why your friends think the domestic violence law doesn't make sense. That it's not equitable," she says.

"I don't know. I already told you what happened. That girl was like twice the size of that poor man, I swear."

She is patient with me.

"Imagine two guys are fighting outside a bar because one of them looked at the other the wrong way," she says to me.

"How wrong?"

"Very wrong."

"OK."

"What do you do?"

"Depends on their size. If they're small, I'd try to separate them. If I think I'll end up getting hit, I'll mind my own business."

"Why?"

"I don't know. Because it's between them."

"All right. Now imagine those two guys are fighting outside a bar because one of them is a faggot and the other one hates faggots. Is that the same thing?"

"No, of course not."

"Why?"

"Because it's not a trivial fight. It's an act of hate."

"And should hating faggots be a crime?"

"Yeah, fuck yeah. Because they're playing with a disadvantage. At least a disadvantage in *this* world. Fascists still insult them and hit them as if there were no faggot fascists. In some countries they're persecuted. Punished by death. And here they had to be closeted until very recently. My father always said that the worst thing that could happen to him in this life was to have a fag for a son—imagine. I think it's our duty to intervene to make homophobia disappear, even if we have to take a few punches."

"Would you say we live in a homophobic society?"

"Well. Less and less so. Where are you going with this?"

"Relax. I'm getting there. Question: Do you believe we live in a society that hates women?"

"No. I wouldn't say it in those words."

"You don't believe we live in a society where women suffer persecution, harassment, mistreatment, insults, discrimination in the workplace, or any other fucked-up shit you can imagine, just for being women?"

"Probably."

"Probably?"

"OK. Yes. Women are discriminated against."

"Do you want me to give you some examples, you chauvinistic pig?"

"No, there's no need. You know I've gone to a ton of lectures. I'm very aware that women are at a disadvantage."

"Perfect. So if a man hits a woman, or mistreats her in some way, in a patriarchal, sexist culture like ours, where women are playing with worse cards than men just for being women, isn't that the same as a homophobe hitting a fag?"

"Can you make the question shorter? I think you're mistaking me for the examining board for your thesis."

"Don't you think our culture considers women inferior to men?"

"Yes."

"And don't you think that considering us inferior forces men, consciously or unconsciously, to put us in our place?"

"And what place is that?"

"It's obvious: behind you all."

In other words: invisible, silenced, ignored. Touché.

Najwa devours me. She turns my arguments against me, explaining how our collective imagination operates on individuals. Movies and songs, advertising, popular culture, it's all impregnated with the same ideology: the girl, the mother, the wife;

in every medium, a successful woman is news just for being a woman, not for her merits; the analysis of female public figures is always accompanied by a review of their beauty, outfits, and personal life. And this is just a superficial look at the problem. One basic example: high heels are uncomfortable, and yet they are almost required at certain events, which forces many women to carry a pair of flats in their little purses, like secret ballerinas, to relieve their feet when the party allows. And there are hundreds of examples like that. Ideology on top of ideology on top of ideology.

"The framework is more subtle than before, but just as efficient," she says to me.

And I feel that she's right, that everything she's saying is true, but—for that same reason—I don't want to keep listening to it, it's irritating me, making me feel bad about myself. And not just about myself but about my family, my friends, my colleagues at work. Her words weigh on me like judgments, and annoy me, because I just want to look at her ass and squeeze it and give it a few little slaps, leave a small pink stretch mark on each cheek and not think, not think about any of this, keep being as blind as I was before, not question myself, live in peace, be a happy, shortsighted, cynical man; a clown; a faithful dog; a domesticated cock; a semen syringe; maybe take a couple of dirty pics for my personal consumption. But I don't want to belong to her pack, not that, not ever; the structural dissatisfaction seems unbearable. I don't want to pay attention, I want to keep ignoring the existence of the culture of silence, of rape, of disdain. I want to know I'm in the right, not have to choose sides. What a drag to have to think about these things. What a drag to have to reexamine my privilege.

But I have to do something, I know it. I have no choice.

6

MY MOTHER SMOKES like she's on death row, and that's one of the only reasons I go visit her every once in a while. Her house is the last bar where you can smoke, which is great, but her emotional intensity and her Olympic ability to jump from one subject to the next sets me off-balance, which is less great.

One comes here to listen and pray in silence, like in church.

"Have you spoken to your sister lately? I don't know what she's expecting out of life, honestly. Every week she's got a new boyfriend. Well, "boyfriends" is what I end up calling them, because not even she can remember their names. She's thirty years old! I've lost all hope that you'll give me grandchildren, but I'm still holding out with her... What do I have to do to get her to make me a grand-mother? I'd take care of everything, the diapers, the food, everything. Of course, when she makes up her mind it'll be too late, and then I'll have to put up with her regrets. Because one day she'll want to be a mother, I'm sure of it, and then I'll wash my hands of the whole thing, she better not dare come crying to me, because Lord knows I've told her every way I know how: find a man, have kids soon, because later life gets more complicated... And she pays me no mind. She never listens to me. Not that you do. But I'm twice her age, and a woman and a mother, I must know something about how these things work. And don't go asking the fisherman about it, it seems like he doesn't care about anything, but that's not the case. He doesn't talk much, but I can tell. He's worried too."

"The fisherman" is my father. Ever since he retired, he spends his weekends on the river, with a couple of his buddies, fishing. Or that's what he claims. Amen.

"You can't imagine how much your cousin's driving me up a tree. Turns out she and her wise-ass husband have signed up for dance classes right nearby, three nights a week. I don't know if it's ballroom dance or jazz or some other stupid thing. And, of course, since I'm close by and have noth-ing better to do, because everyone assumes I have nothing better to do, they asked me to take care of their kid those evenings. Three evenings a week. And I love the kid, but since he's started walking he's a real pain in the ass, running all over the house, moving everything, breaking everything. When it's not raining, I take him down to the park so he can burn off some energy, and then he's calm, but still, he never stops, he's like that Tasmanian Devil. He hits other kids, and then I'm the one who has to apologize to the parents. And I'm not even his grandmother. I'm sick of it. Any day now I'll tell them to stick that boy where the sun don't shine."

I know my cousin's son, and he's just a normal kid. From what I've been told, at his age I *was* hell on wheels, the kinda kid who's discovered the secret pleasure of kicking adults in their shins under the table and on elevators. A "handful," as they say. But I suppose my mother doesn't remember that, or doesn't want to remember it. Amen.

"And now your sister tells me that she's thinking of going to Canada for a year. Canada, I swear! What's in Canada? She already knows how to speak English...And French! She still acts like she's fifteen years old, and everything is all just going out with her friends and coming home in a sorry state. You know what I was doing at fifteen? Working. Working to help out my family, and if there was anything left over, sure, I'd go out. But only on Saturdays, and only until ten, and if I was any later, you know your grandfather, he'd be waiting for me with the belt. You know how he was. A diamond in the rough. When I wanted to study nursing the guidance counselor said it was a tough road, that hardly anyone made it through, and your grandfather agreed with him, and between the two of them, I gave up on that dream. But he did that for me. I probably wouldn't have been good at being a nurse, and he was the one who got me the job at the hardware store."

I've always wondered what would have happened if my mother had gone to a school with a competent guidance counselor, instead of a mentally deficient one. Amen.

"But thank goodness your father showed up when he did, because your grandfather had a very short fuse, and he didn't like the skirts I wore. It was like a rescue. What does your sister need to go to Canada for? Doesn't she have friends here? Aren't there handsome men here? Doesn't she have a job here? Sure, I went to a new city at nineteen, but that was because I got married, and at twenty I already had you, and at twenty-four your sister, and while your father worked I took care of the house and you kids, and that's it, the house and you guys and coffee with my friends, until you left home and your sister left home, ay, that was so hard on me, and then what? If it weren't for your father, even though sometimes I wished he wasn't around, then what? Because I've never wanted for anything, let the record state. Your father made me feel safe. And what is your sister expecting from life? Does she want to be single at my age? Because now it's easy for her to meet someone, go to bed with him, enjoy. She's young and pretty. She's smart. But that doesn't last forever. She's nearly too old to have kids! When is she finally going to make me a grandmother? When?"

My mother's homily awakens my desire to grab her by her jacket lapels and shake her until she wakes up. It used to be, years ago, that I found her a bit sad, a woman tormented by a lack of am-bition, bored of looking at herself in the mirror. Now she seems like an angry woman. Cranky. A woman whose indignation is one step away from anarchy. And she doesn't seem to know why, even after some soul-searching. Although she probably has her suspicions. She suspects that her life has been a disaster from start to finish; that she never had a real opportunity to do something, anything, on her own merits; that she went from daughter to wife to mother at a shockingly terrible speed, as did so many of her generation. She suspects that. What she perhaps doesn't know is that she was tricked. That they made her believe that being a mother and a wife and a homeowner was her dream, that my father was her Prince Charming, that having us was her purpose in life. That that was it, and that she had no further aspirations throbbing in her veins. They tricked her by mythologizing a life that would always leave her on the margins, like a pariah. Because the important things are never on the margins, are they? Amen.

"Sorry, Son. I'm getting worked up. Go on, tell me about you. What's new in your life? How's work going?"

I wonder what to do. Should I tell her what I'm thinking? I have no right. Do I tell her that I feel she's been scammed? Do I tell her that maybe it's too late for her, but that she shouldn't wish on her daughter, my sister, the same sermon they sold her almost sixty years ago? Or should I keep my mouth shut? And be a coward, a complicit coward. Maybe it's better to let her sleepwalk through life, unaware, unconscious, asleep. To maintain the inertia of six decades rolling in the same direction. Maybe it's better to keep the wool over her eyes, in case the truth is too much to bear. The red pill or the blue pill.

"Have you seen *The Matrix*, Mom?" I ask her.

"No, never. Your father likes that kind of movie. You know my favorite is *Young Bess*, about the Virgin Queen. It's so beautiful, so romantic."

The fucking Virgin Queen, seriously? My head is about to explode.

What would a good feminist do?

7

TEN COMMANDMENTS OF A GOOD FEMINIST

A good feminist does not need to say he is a
feminist.

A good feminist does not consume cultural
products that denigrate women.

A good feminist does not participate in
activities that invisibilize women.

A good feminist does not tell a woman what
she must do.

A good feminist does not interrupt a woman
when she is speaking.

A good feminist does not pity a woman for
her historical burdens.

A good feminist has no prejudices against
menstrual blood.

A good feminist does not defend the idea that
there are essential differences between
men and women.

A good feminist is always a feminist, on
every occasion.

A good feminist does not back down.

8

I DON'T CALL first when I go over to Najwa's house anymore. I did it for a while, even after she gave me a set of keys, because I didn't want to abuse her trust. It's not "our" house, it's hers: with her rules, her layout, her routines, and her habits. But after a while she asked me to stop acting like a guest, told me there was no need for me to announce my visits since I was already a part of her life and had the right to come and go as I pleased—just so long as I always respected three conditions:

1. Cohabitation doesn't mean being together all the time. She needs her space, not only to work, but also to exist. It goes without saying that I do too. Standard greetings are permitted, but a closed door is one that

should not be opened without the consent of the person inside.

2. The bathroom, kitchen, and living room are common spaces. Since there is only one television, if someone wants to use it they have veto rights over and above whoever is occupying the same space for other activities, such as reading.

3. Cleaning chores should be handled according to common sense, and not some strict administrative calendar, except for in the bedroom, where she maintains the prerogative to control the chaos levels.

I enter the house and hear moaning.

Actually it's not just moaning. I also hear screaming and hitting.

All the lights are out, except in the bedroom. According to the first rule, if the bedroom door is open I can go in without asking permission. I am an intruder with unlimited access. I approach slowly, without making noise. She didn't hear me come in, I don't think, but I understand that she knows I could come in at any point.

I peek inside the room. I want to surprise her, give her a start. I behave like the stealthiest ghost in the neighborhood. My cock stirs.

Najwa is lying on the bed, on her back, with her legs open and her hands inside her panties. She is masturbating while watching lesbian porn. On the screen, a gagged woman with her arms tied to a post and her legs separated by a wooden rectangle, maybe a bench, is being whipped by another girl, both in their very early twenties. The ass of the girl on the receiving end is covered with red-and-purple marks. I see Najwa squirming and closing her eyes, and I decide to wait to show myself until after she's climaxed. She stretches. She pulls her hands out of her panties but keeps watching the video.

"Hello, gorgeous," I say.

She barely bats an eyelash. She turns her head toward me, with a placid smile, and gestures for me to come over and kiss her.

"Hellooooo," she says.

She seems high, but she isn't. She's always like that after an intense orgasm. The scene arouses me, and as I kiss her I undo my belt and pants. I don't think any foreplay is needed, and she isn't usually interested in that sort of heavy petting before sex anyway. I take off my shirt and stroke my cock through my underwear. I carefully move aside the laptop computer, despite how bad I want to tear off her clothes. It's a Mac. Then I focus on her pussy.

After a few well-studied positions and a couple of clitoral orgasms, she asks me to hit her. It's not the first time we've done that. She turns over, buries her head in the pillow and lifts her ass slightly.

"With the paddle or my hands?"

"Your hands," she exhales.

The paddle leaves terrible marks, and I'm sure the pain is commensurate with its signature. It's not a toy to be used regularly. She chooses. So I'll use my hands.

I take off my three rings: two on my left, one on my right.

And I begin.

The intensity and duration of the beating is not negotiated, it unfolds intuitively. I have to remain attentive to her breathing, her screams, the movement of her body. She generally can handle two or three blows on each side, but it's not an exact science. Sometimes she wants me to stop; sometimes she wants me to keep going. In either case, she tells me.

I usually end up with swollen, aching hands. I've even taken it so far that I couldn't put back on some of my rings, because my fingers were so inflamed. I execute each smack like a scientific procedure: I lift my hand, I calculate the angle, I fix on the site of impact, feint, and determine the strength of the blow. It's not the same to use your palm as the back of your hand. It's not the same near the tailbone as on the fleshier, softer area. My erection grows the more she screams and the more I see her convulse on the bed. I don't always last until the end: certain gestures spur me on, and I stop hitting her, open her legs and sink my cock suddenly as deep inside her as I can. I normally don't go back to wrecking her ass after penetrating her, unless she asks me to. We both tacitly assume that I will always get excited, and so the type of sex we have depends on what she desires.

I tell her I want to ejaculate in her mouth. She nods.

When we're finished, I'm exhausted. I lie on my back, looking up at the ceiling, trying to catch my breath and lower my heart rate. I can feel my left hand throbbing and I imagine her ass tomorrow, bruised, deformed, something she'd have to hide at the beach. It's not an image that makes me happy, even though I know that everything's fine between us. I feel confused.

Later, smoking a cigarette in the kitchen, because we don't like to smoke where we sleep, I tell her about my visit to my mother's, and I explain my doubts. She thinks it over, she isn't sure. I take advantage of the fact that her guard's down to question her about a few contradictions I've noticed.

"You like high heels, which are a historical symbol of control over the female body. You like sadomasochistic lesbian porn; in fact, you even like me to hit you. You like wedding rings, a vintage vestige of romantic love that could even be interpreted as a sign of enslavement. You like *rancheras* and tangos, which are filled with crimes against women and female betrayals and gloomy spinsters. You like to show serious cleavage. I like it too, but I'm starting to feel disgusted, and ashamed, about all those things, and I'm just a rookie at all this. I can't stand how hard it makes me to hit you with the paddle, but I can't stop thinking about the comic books I used to read, with tied-up women, spanking...Can you help me? My cock is at odds with my ideology."

She takes a long drag. Exhales slowly.

"I'm not in control of my desires," she says.

Now I'm the one who smokes. Her eyeglasses rest on the table. She continues.

"I don't freely choose the things I choose. I've been taught to love high heels, and tangos, and rings. I've discovered that the paddling makes me feel alive, and that watching other women get whipped turns me on. The first thing you have to remember is that I am aware of it all. I know that I'm a product of my generation and of the patterns that shape my desire. I know I'm not free."

I try to fit her reasoning into the complex architectural system I've spent months constructing.

"And what about the other part?"

"There's a difference between the public sphere and the private one. It's not the same thing to be in front of a microphone as it is to be talking to my friends, or writing an article versus my personal, private experiences. I'm infected with it, but I've been lucky enough, or capable enough, to realize that. I can't renounce my desire. But I can denounce the ideology that allows people like me to exist. Or people like you, who get hard when you hit my ass and see it get red. Have you ever stopped to think that maybe it goes beyond the erotic comics you read as a kid? Ask *yourself* where it all comes from, instead of asking me, asshole. You didn't jerk off to Wonder Woman: you were turned on by the idea of control, even before you knew what control was. It doesn't excite you to hit me. What excites you is imagining that you're the one who gets to decide when to stop hitting me."

I don't even feel like smoking anymore. I wonder if I'd have been able to realize all these things if I hadn't met her. And if the answer is no, what does that say about me?

"I love high heels, but if I have a daughter I'll never tell her that they make her look more beautiful," she says.

I look at her glasses. They are right in the middle of the room.

9

SEEING THE WORLD from this new perspective is overwhelming.

I detect male microaggressions everywhere, all the time: in movies, in how all the world leaders are men and their wives are eternally supportive; in the offhand comments my friends make about "helping"—that verb!—around the house and with their own kids; on the radio, online, in editorials written by journalists I respect; in the way people sit on the benches in the square, in the relationships between clerks and customers, in the way telephone salesmen treat me. It's even worse at work: a couple of conversations around the coffee machine and a series of articles about the glass ceiling female journalists face are the last straw. I start to look at my boss as a tyrant, and I decide to take a leave before I lose my head and make a mistake. Since I've always been an optimist, and good-natured, the classic protorevolutionary who dreams of a better, more just world, I am surprised to now be constantly pissed off.

I read a Twitter thread that explains why feminism doesn't seek pure equality between men and women. I have trouble understanding it, because of the condensing implicit in that format, but I do come away with something: equality is utopian, because it isn't enough to level the playing field in terms of rights when women still bear the burdens of centuries of punishment, entire generations flattened. The women are rapeseed: we've lubricated the machinery with their oil. That's why we still need to compensate with quotas, with positive discrimination, with specific laws. Someone mentions Iris Marion Young and her theory on structural injustices and the shared responsibility for remedying them. I search for her online. Equality will be a logical consequence of our ability to crush those heavy burdens, but we all have to take responsibility. I reinterpret that in my own way: whoever isn't in favor of affirmative legislation is either an idiot or comes from the future.

I retweet.

My head itches. I think it's stress. I draw vaginas with colored pens and then hang them up strategically, so my roommates will see them: on the bathroom mirror, inside the cabinet where we keep the dishes, on the back of the TV near the HDMI input. I do it because, according to Freud, we men have an atavistic fear of that part of the female body. Najwa told me a legend about a barbarian town that hoisted flags emblazoned with vagina drawings when they entered combat, because the image terrified their adversaries into paralysis. I don't know if it's true, but I've appropriated the concept. My roommates tear down the drawings every night. I put them back up early in the morning.

As the weeks pass my drawings improve, with more detail and nuance. I flirt with hyperrealism. The hyperrealism makes them scream.

Daily news stories seem increasingly more absurd and less interesting. I'm a nonconformist sponge. I continue my leave of absence due to a fake flu with a leave of absence for my fake wrist sprain, so I have a lot of free time. I read about the war between East and West, about workers' fight against capital, about the protests for and against a series of political prisoners. The world is a dystopia and it bores me to tears. My war is elsewhere.

My roommates lack creativity. If I were them, I would counterattack with drawings of enormous, hairy penises, covered in veins. Or take it even further: add an extra ball, moustaches and pipes, like elegant gentlemen. Their lack of imagination forces me to intensify my efforts. I cover the walls with extraordinary, uncanonical, aesthetically subversive vaginas. I manage to get them to step up their game: now they not only tear off my drawings, but they leave a pile of ashes in front of my door. Their initiative is so childish it's ridiculous.

I read about femicides in Mexico. About gender-related violence in Europe. About discrimination toward women in the Arab world. The numbers are dizzying. I internalize common neologisms to use in debates. Mansplaining: when a man believes he has to explain something to a woman because, being a woman, she must not know it. Manspreading: when a man opens his legs and takes up more space than he should. Manattributing: when a woman says something at a panel discussion and then another panelist repeats it and attributes it to a man. I, dictionary.

Najwa and I keep sleeping together and talking. I find myself defending a basic idea: the only real battle of the 21st century is the women's fight. That's the wound of the world. I see it so clearly that it's frightening. The 19th century was the century of class struggle; the 20th, of ethnic minorities. Of course, we're still trying to win those wars, but no Western government, today, would dare to question them. Najwa smiles: she can see the effect she's had on me. I make a decision from which there is no going back: to become a troll.

My handle on social networks is @feminassti. It's not a brilliant play on words, but it allows me a certain anonymity. I consider using my own name. I come to the conclusion that the character will have more potency if their gender, age, social class, and level of education are left unclear. And I don't want to feel censored by the threat of losing my job, because I want to be cruel, ferocious, a real troublemaker. Even though I was starting to fear that, with all the days of work I'd missed, they were already looking for my replacement. When I think about that, I realize I don't care. I have some savings. I can allow myself to air my opinions online for a while.

In fact, I don't even want to air my opinions. I want to cause pain.

My first tweet is subtle:

@feminassti
Men, you don't know it, but we're at war.
Women want our fucking heads on pikes.

To get attention, I start following widely: declared feminists; left-wing and right-wing journalists; well-known Spanish machos; comedians, intellectuals, and writers both male and female; Nazis; soccer players. I know this is a long-distance race, and I force myself to tweet an average of fifty times a day. Insistence by accumulation.

> @feminassti
> If you only feel sorry for women when they're dead it's because you aren't into necrophilia.

> @feminassti
> Pussy's switching sides.

> @feminassti
> As far as you're concerned, my PMS lasts 12 months a year. You've been warned.

Gradually, the first insults start to trickle in. Perseverance is an art. I go from fifty followers to a hundred, from a hundred to a thousand in a week. Women insult me too, but I was expecting that: half of my tweets are more misandrist than feminist, I've completely ignored the queer universe, and the character I've adopted isn't likable. I don't know if it helps the cause, but I unceremoniously attack a ton of extremely centrist male chauvinists. As a test, I follow all the women in my family, concealing the relationships by also following a hundred strangers. Sometimes I tag them. One of my cousins blocks me. My mother, on the other hand, retweets me. Especially when I'm very crude. She never adds anything of her own to the retweets.

@feminassti
Less semen in porn and more flaccid dicks.
Sexual realism.

Najwa doesn't know what I'm doing, even though she is one of my more than three thousand followers. I get about fifty threats a day, including murder, rape, and sudden death. Most public figures have blocked me. I guess I'm playing in a rough league. Some women write me private messages politely asking me to tone down my comments, saying that I'm not helping the feminist cause; other celebrate my wit and sting, and encourage me to keep fighting. A blog asks to interview me, but I refuse.

My roommates leave me a letter in my bedroom. They say they don't want to keep living with me and offer me two options: move, in which case they'll cover my next share of the rent and give me back my deposit out of their own pockets; or stay in the apartment, as the lease grants me the right to, alone, in which case they would not pay the next month's rent or expenses. My response was to replace the vaginas with menstrual blood. Actually it's not menstrual blood, but tampons stained with red paint that I place around the house: in the kitchen sink, the toilet bowl, the silverware drawer, the sofa. Generic brand. The tampons advertised on TV are, given the state of my bank account, incredibly expensive.

I'm not a total pig: I waited until the paint was dry first.

I have five thousand followers, and one of them informed the police about a tweet I received demanding my rape, followed by an acid bath. The police contacted me and told me that maybe I'm being too aggressive, and asked if I wanted to file a formal complaint. The Community Manager used the word *agresiva*, ending with an a, and I was surprised, because I'd been extremely careful to not write a single tweet that defined me as someone who considers themself female. So I assume that everyone thinks that @feminassti is a woman.

That same day I create a survey:

Can a man be a feminist?
  a) No
  b) Yes
  c) No, but he can support the cause

The first option wins by 83 percent.

I stop tweeting for twenty-four hours.

10

NAJWA'S MOVED into my apartment, which is bigger than hers, and I discovered that my crusade is useless.

@feminassti has almost ten thousand followers, and an average of fifty likes and more than a thousand retweets a day. I maintain a routine of daily tweets, apart from the responses I allow myself and the private messages. A national newspaper included me among the most active and combative feminists on Twitter. I keep refusing interviews.

In any case, I've achieved nothing, except a bit of noise and the feeling that there are a lot of women who share my ideas and a lot who don't. I talk about it with Najwa. I'd lied and told her I was now working from home, so she wouldn't find me out, but she now responds clairvoyantly:

"It doesn't matter what we do. Social media isn't the real world, it's just a way to vent, a bar you can leave anytime, with no consequences. Academia, of which I'm a part, hunkers down in such abstract discourse that people can't understand it. Some contemporary feminist postures are so naive they make you want to burn T-shirts, and others are so complicated that people give up on finding the energy to understand them. Try to explain Judith Butler on TV, while the politician of the moment interrupts you. Feminists fight among themselves when it comes to complex subjects like prostitution and porn. Some are even afraid to publicly define themselves as feminists, because they worry they'll be associated with radical ideas. When asked, they respond: "It depends on what you mean by 'feminist.'" It depends? Fuck off, bitch. What the hell does it depend on? Feminism is the only social advancement that has spent decades on the margins. The patriarchy has done its job well, impeccably, in fact. We are the biggest minority in the world, and the most ignored. Except when they kill us, of course. Then everyone supports our position. For a little while. For as long as the prime-time news segment lasts."

Najwa isn't particularly succinct.

"The only good thing I can say is that our revolution is the only peaceful one ever. That's why it moves so slowly."

And while she speaks, my mother's face superimposes itself onto hers, along with the frozen faces of my Twitter followers, and in all of them I recognize a repeating paradigm, the sketch of a mathematical problem that just needs one or two formulas to be solvable. The grammar of a language. I see it intuitively, and if I can name it, I can make it real. What are the physical symptoms of rage?

Raised voice.

Fixed stare.

Bared teeth.

Accelerated muscular response.

Rapid heartbeat.

The women around me are filled with anger. It's not a spontaneous anger born of some fleeting dissatisfaction, of an immediate desire being thwarted, but an interior, organic rage, contained by hundreds of routines. An anger accepted as a natural state, itemized in chapters of minor angers that temporarily alleviate its condensation. Anger as a mental illness that doesn't count. Concealed with makeup. Mitigated with medications: opioids, antidepressants, illegal drugs. Statistics say that women are the segment of the population with the highest rate of prescription drug consumption.

Lorazepam, diazepam, bromazepam. I commend my soul to your hands.

@feminassti
How many of us have had it up to here?

I tell Najwa that I have to go down and get some smokes. I'm lying: I have an unopened pack in my bag.

I go out onto the street and call my mother. I ask her if she's mad.

"At who? Your father?" she says.

Subtext.

"No. In general. I don't know, at the world."

She says no. That she's at home with my cousin's son and doesn't have time to think about that kind of stuff. That the kid is trying to eat the door to the kitchen. She asks me if I'm OK. I reformulate.

"If you were eighteen years old now, what would you like to do?"

She thinks it over.

"Everything I haven't done," she tells me.

And she makes a list.

Go out three nights a week.
Travel around Europe.
Go to college.
Have a lot of boyfriends.

Have my first baby ten years later.
Learn languages.
Have my own income.
Improvise.

My followers tell me that yes, they've had it up to here. My phone is exploding with notifications. I break my own record: five thousand replies, almost as many retweets. I'm a virus. The numbers keep climbing.

Then I get an idea for an experiment.

11

MY COUSIN'S SON is climbing onto the back of the sofa so he can do a belly flop onto the other sofa. The living room floor is covered in crushed crayons, water, and tissues covered in boogers. My mother is on her knees, trying to clean a blue stain off the rug. According to my experience with the first tampons, it's not going to be easy to remove. I see that she's sweating.

"Arturo, your shoes..."

After chasing him for a while in a useless attempt to keep him from destroying the sofas, she tried to negotiate with him: Yes, OK, he can keep jumping but only if he takes off his shoes, we've been out on the street and who knows what you've stepped in. Animal poo, mud, trash. The boy responded, in his own way, that he couldn't agree. That without shoes he didn't have the right grip.

I do nothing. It's a struggle, I'll admit, because I'd like to grab him by the legs, toss him over my shoulder and lock him in the bathroom so I could talk to my mother in peace, but in the end his presence works in my favor. I've come here with a plan, and the chaos can help me achieve my goals.

"It's so beautiful what you're doing, Mom," I tell her.

She looks at me, still kneeling, from below. I sit down on a chair.

"What's so beautiful?"

I wait, wanting to do this right.

"All of this. Taking care of Arturo. Taking care of all of us, really. Putting your life in the service of what's really important, entertaining us, feeding us. When I was little, oh..."

No. Don't get nostalgic. Try another tactic.

"I mean that I can't imagine a more satisfying job than yours. Than women's. Watching us grow up from the very beginning, seeing us learn to talk, to walk, even to jump from one sofa to the other, like Arturo. Seeing us get bigger, slowly, day by day, year after year. I imagine that sometimes it's a bit of a sacrifice, I don't know, not sleeping in, barely having time for anything besides keeping the house in order. But the house is the home, and the home is the center of our lives, of our family. I think we envy you all."

She stands up.

"What? Who does?"

"We do. You know, men. We couldn't do what you do. It isn't in our blood. Our bodies are always demanding that we be out and about, wilding with our friends. We're savages. That's why we admire women. That's why we love you all. Haven't you heard men say 'I like all women'? Of course you have. You can carry a child inside you for nine months, and give birth to him, and take care of him all his life. That's something wonderful, I can't even imagine it. And everything that happens afterward: the diapers, school, the park... You devote your lives to giving others' life. What could be better than that?"

She opens her mouth as if to say something. I don't let her.

"And what can I say about my grandparents? You take care of them too. I remember Grandpa's final years, when he couldn't walk anymore and he couldn't control his sphincter. And there you were, every day, cleaning him, changing his diapers, cooking his food. And then you'd come rushing back home to cook for us and Dad, we were only home for a quick lunch; and when we came back at night everything was tidy and dinner was on the table. What incredible devotion, what love. Really: what love. A man would have hired a caretaker, or two, one for Grandpa, and a house cleaner too. Knowing us, the cleaner would probably be young and very pretty, something good to look at. But not you. No, you were born for this, you're genetically prepared for caretaking."

Even though there's a little boy there, who's now decided to use the sofa as a trampoline, my mother lights a cigarette. I think it's the first time she's ever lit up in front of him. She takes a long drag and exhales a cloud of smoke in the kid's direction. Arturo coughs.

"The best part is you do it without complaining. I guess it's because it comes so naturally to you. I'm not saying women are submissive, of course. Maybe it's that you're...dependent. Not specifically on men's money and work, which is possible too, but mostly dependent on this way of life. You need to care for others because for you it's like breathing. It's your oxygen, and we all need oxygen. That's why I say you're dependent."

"Look, Son..."

"Don't interrupt me, Mom. Please. I'm talking. From my heart. The other day you told me that you would have liked to have kids later in life, go to college, all that shit. Why? Why go to college when your birthright is the best job in the world? Take it from me, I went to college and partied hundreds of times. Sure, you learn a lot in college and you meet people. And you can study abroad, if you can afford it. But then what? Look for work like a dumbass, accept shit salaries to pay your dues, running around like crazy. It was horrible, I swear, when I started living on my own and throwing parties at my place, parties that everybody came to, and then I'd get up in the morning and realize that the house doesn't clean itself. And learning to iron my own shirts. It was horrible. We had it so good here, all of us, with you. If I could be born again I'd always stay by your side, so you could take care of me. And I think you were very brave to make the decision to get pregnant so young. Women today take their time, they want to live, or that's what they say. Live? You're the one who's had a real life. You were so young that now you could take care of your grandkids, if you had any. Isn't that what you want? Shit, you were so young you could even take care of your great-grandkids. The world of women is so beautiful, Mom."

I pause. I want to see how she responds. Arturo says he's hungry and smoking is bad. Since we aren't paying attention to him, he screams it. Over and over, like a prayer.

"Give that kid something to eat, see if that'll shut him up. And make me something too while you're at it. I was writing an article this morning and didn't have time to shop for food. But something elaborate, alright? Something delicious. I'm in no hurry."

My mother smashes out the cigarette in an ashtray. She doesn't just put it out, she pulverizes it. I think she needs support.

"When I think of you I always imagine you in the kitchen. And that makes me hungry."

And...she explodes. At first the words don't come out, she is so furious she can only manage to articulate unfinished phrases. She stutters. I look at her condescendingly.

"Mom, don't speak to me in Womanese. You know we men can't understand it. Are you going to make our snacks?"

Her eyes fog over. I was expecting her cheeks to turn red—something cliché, literary—but instead her face grows dark. Not like addicts or people with liver problems, but as if suddenly she'd sprouted a splotchy birthmark, the irregular bark on an olive tree, a mask.

No, that's not it: I think she actually vomited up a mask.

Just then her throat opens and she begins to scream. To scream at me. She spews a chain of insults, curses, lists of disappointments, shattered dreams, reproaches of unknown origin, threats, ingrown pain. She paces around the living room, moving objects. She grabs a framed photo. She lifts it up. She puts it back in its place. She observes it. She moves it to another spot. She observes it again. She throws it against the wall. The boy is crying, nonstop. She continues screaming expletives, she tries to light a cigarette but ends up breaking it. She lights another. She tells the kid to shut up or she'll smack him upside the head, in those words; she points a finger at me, coming very close; I can feel her saliva ricocheting off my forehead; she is talking to me, but without me, I mean, as if I were a microphone, anyone, a sounding board. She recalls dramas from her childhood, youth, and early married years, and I have nothing to say in response. She stretches like a serpent. The boy's crying has turned into hysteria, he is completely out of control, rolling around on the floor and dirtying his clothes with crushed crayon. He's a total mess. My mother looks at him coldly, and I have the impression—for a microsecond—that she is going to stomp on his head. In the end she picks him up from the floor, by the shirt, roughly. I see Arturo's small legs swaying in the air. I didn't know my mother had the strength.

She opens the front door, with the boy still suspended in the air.

She deposits him outside, like a bag of garbage.

She comes back in.

She slams the door.

She stares at me. Her chest puffs up, then deflates. I can't hear her heart rate, but I can imagine it. She takes a long drag.

"And Arturo?" I dare to ask.

She releases the smoke.

"The doorman can deal with him," she says, then adds, "You want some wine? I've got some things to explain to you."

I am thirty-five, and this is the first time I've ever seen my mother depart from the script. My legs are shaking. Arturo is screaming on the other side of the door, scared to death.

I don't feel guilty: I have just become a soldier.

PART

TWO

12

WHEN I'M ON the lookout for recruits, I introduce myself as Garbo. Hardly anyone asks where the name comes from: they understand that it's short for Gabriel or a version of my surname, and when they insist on finding out where it comes from I just say "everybody calls me that." This false identity allows me to circumvent the enormous ethical gap in my task, because a soldier is not a man, he is someone new, someone else: a flesh tool in service to a cause, a butler who never asks questions, nature's indifferent gaze, unaware of the meaning of the word *instinct*. In other words: as Garbo, I am no longer myself.

Garbo chooses places with high levels of testosterone, like gyms, bars in the wee hours, and restaurants near male-dominated places of work:

courts, banks, construction sites. Internet forums or friendship apps don't work, because he needs to see the real faces of the future members of his group. Their vehemence and their rage. If this is a war, he needs an army.

He focuses on uncommon targets, extraordinary men able to sacrifice their time and their safety for an ideal world where they can feel at home. Men educated in a superlative historical misogyny, burdened with rancor and fears, with frustrations and resentment. Men who exude superiority every time a woman crosses their path, men who instantly intuit whether the effort of humiliating her is worth it or not, and for whom that effort is always rewarded with satisfaction and a good night's sleep. Such extreme stereotypes that they would only seem realistic in the world of nonfiction, like Donald Trump. Garbo wants men who reason with a pre-democratic logic, not only with the certainty that men and women are different, but that bestowing equal rights to both sexes was a mistake: since there is a biological hierarchy that challenges that *tabula rosa*, any progress made by women is nothing more than a fraud achieved in societies with meek men, products of hunger and poverty, drug-addled hippies, dreamers blind to reality, cowardly dogs heeling to an imaginary constitution.

Garbo is patient and observant.

Hugo is a social worker and a committed anti-racist activist. Garbo meets him in a low-lit pub at three in the morning, after a woman threw a drink in his face and he licked his lips as he asked her if she enjoyed squirting.

"Wet and wild," says Garbo.

Hugo looks at him warily, trying to figure out if he's joking or flirting. Garbo smiles at him and lies, "I tried it with her earlier. What a cunt. I don't know who she thinks she is. You want a drink? I'll buy, in solidarity."

When he isn't protesting on behalf of ethnic minorities and facing up to neo-Nazis who defend segregation, Hugo spends his time watching porn. No one pays him to, but they could. His favorites are the "black Chinese girls," as he calls them. Afro-Asians with big tits and big lips, but thin waists and "brown sugar" skin. He is overweight and too hairy, but that doesn't stop him from wearing tight, short-sleeved shirts. He oozes self-confidence. For him, women are tissues to ejaculate into, and that's why he has no qualms about telling them what he wants to do to them, and how and for how long, just seconds after introducing himself. He's an expert in bizarre sexual practices. He thinks relationships are a trap, a covert castration strategy, and he has been proudly single since eighteen—a symbol of independence. His penis, his flag.

"I jerk off three or four times a day. Every day," he says.

Garbo gets him drunk. He uses the conversations with his former roommates as bait, and as proof of his authority. He makes up unconfessable zoophilic secrets and carefully jots down Hugo's recommendations on the dark web, with interest. Hugo feels he's found a twin brother. Before they say good night, they exchange numbers and joke about what they would do to the woman who rejected them if they ran into her. Nothing good.

Over the next few days they keep up a constant routine of text messages, mostly with links to classic porn videos, obligatory viewing for them to start to understand each other, and to new sites, with heretofore unpublished material; they also talk about personal subjects: work, vacations, the virtues of being single. They get together sometimes on the weekends to talk like old friends. On one of those nights, Garbo confesses that he's trying to put together a group.

"A group? What for?" asks Hugo.

"To put women in their place."

Hugo is thrilled by the idea. He has a privileged, multitasking mind, the product of years of experience handling and sharing files in different formats, and he can think of hundreds of actions to carry out. Garbo discusses the methods and strategies. Between the two of them they plan out possible scenarios and the consequences of a hypothetical intervention. They take notes so they won't forget a detail. They conclude that the group needs at least four other members, and they decide to start recruiting that very night.

When Garbo gets home, he showers with boiling-hot water.

13

AS FAR AS Najwa is concerned, I'd joined a science-fiction book club and made new friends. That's the reason why I sometimes come home later than usual, and some Sundays I pull all-nighters, something I'd never done before, considering that almost all my old friends are pretty early to bed since they became fathers. She doesn't mind my absence, and in fact she thinks it's awesome that I go out more often and spend less time in front of the computer, especially because I told her that these new friends are very civilized, very well-read, the typical utopian intellectuals who get drunk quickly and want to solve all the world's problems.

"Your liver will thank you," she tells me.

I don't mention that I've quit my job, that I'm surviving thanks to my life savings and am ineligible for unemployment, because I lost my job for a valid reason: not showing up.

@feminassti
How many times a day do men lie to you?

If only I knew how to explain to her what I'm doing.

Even though I somehow sensed it after trying it out on my mother, I didn't have a clear plan of action until I spoke with Najwa a few weeks before meeting Hugo, while we were lying in bed watching a low-budget horror film. Something she once said was stuck in my head—"Our revolution is the only peaceful one ever. That's why it moves so slowly"—and during a scene where the protagonist, the final survivor of a group massacred by a woodcutter linked to a sect that worshiped grain, was destroying her enemy's face with a shovel, I asked her about violence and women.

"Historically, violence belongs to the male sphere," she told me.

I pointed to the woodcutter's brain slipping like mercury from what must have been his ear. Najwa continued.

"Female violence is associated with monstrosity. Women, according to the canons, are not violent. But at some point, in exceptional circumstances, something clicks in our brains and then we lose it. In a big way. Theoretically, in a bigger way than men do: you murder in a colder way. When we kill, we take it to another level, we do it passionately. Like in *Kill Bill*."

Decapitations, liters of blood, multiple amputations. I get it.

She told me that it probably all originated with the myth of Medea. A powerful, intelligent, talented enchantress who is feared and respected, who because of exile and infidelity decides to exterminate everyone she considers guilty of her fall from grace, and then, as the cherry on top, her own children. In a really brutal way. All to hurt Jason. Najwa pointed out that there was something funny in that the root of Medea's madness was what men had done to her. Once again, they are the protagonists of the story.

"What could be more monstrous than killing your own children?"

From then on, she explained, violence carried out by women has been treated like something abnormal, a trance. A fit of insanity. A violent woman is someone who isn't right in the head, subjected to such high levels of pressure that she loses control and gives in to her basic instincts; ceases to be a person, if she ever was, and becomes a monster. Film and literature have worked hard to disseminate this idea: *I Spit on Your Grave, Friday the 13th . . .* Women kill out of jealousy, revenge, or because they were born crazy. They kill impulsively. Without thinking. Because if they stopped to think, they wouldn't do it.

"Is that why the feminist revolution has been pacifist?" I asked.

"Maybe. But it's not all black or white. There are shades of gray."

"I read that the English suffragettes were pretty dangerous."

"Hah! They sure were. More than the Americans or the Spaniards, at least. Imagine a group of angry hooligans; and now imagine them with ovaries."

"I'm too much of a coward."

"But I was talking about another sort of even-more-violent acts. Ones that have nothing to do with fits of anger."

"Such as?"

"Like Diana the Huntress, the avenger in Ciudad Juárez. You do remember how many women are killed in Mexico, right? Hundreds every year, hundreds of missing or raped girls. Ciudad Juárez is the world's femicide capital, and has been for almost a decade. Well it turns out that after a series of twenty or thirty rapes and murders of girls on their way home on mass transit, a woman decided to investigate. And she came to the conclusion that the guilty parties were, often, the bus drivers themselves."

"That's fucked-up."

"Yup. So she starts to kill them. All the ones she can. According to witnesses, she is a fiftysomething woman who boards the bus and shoots. And then she leaves. That's it. No drama."

I can feel my skepticism unroll, stretch out, and become long, like a reptile.

"That doesn't sound like an episode of temporary insanity."

"Exactly. It's a premeditated, conscious act. She even published an alleged manifesto. Wait, I'll look it up for you... She says, 'I'm an instrument to avenge women, who seem to society to be weak. But we aren't, we're brave, and if we aren't respected, we'll take matters into our own hands. The women of Ciudad Juárez are strong.' It was in all the news outlets."

"And did the rate of femicides go down? I mean, did it work?"

"I doubt it. Killing women is practically a national sport in Mexico. But I am sure that a lot of the drivers who weren't killed, and who were guilty, lived in fear for months. And that they didn't pull their dick out of their pants ever, not even to piss."

Beside the manifesto, on her computer screen, I could see a photograph of one of the murdered girls. I'm terrible at guessing the age of adolescents, but I would've sworn she was just twelve or thirteen. I tried to imagine the man who had raped her and then thrown her body out onto the side of the road, from the bus. It was an ordinary face, a family man, a responsible worker. Perhaps that was when I understood it.

"Don't you think violence is a justifiable way to achieve certain objectives?" I asked.

"Of course. Since the French Revolution, almost every social achievement has come down to blows."

"And why do women insist on fighting the patriarchy so peacefully? I calculate it'll take you three or four centuries at this rate. I don't get it. Did you get together in your coven and take some vote of moderation? Drive slow, arrive alive? Squeeze but don't strangle? I thought the revolution will be feminist, or it will be nothing. Are you going to smash the system politely?"

"It's not that simple, you idiot. It's not like going on strike, or throwing Molotov cocktails at the riot police, or setting up makeshift barricades. We aren't miners, we don't have a union. This is a movement that involves all of society, not just a government or a businessman we can present our demands to. It's a marathon. We have to eliminate every one of the floors that the patriarchy has built on our backs. It's not about blowing up the building and waiting for the rubble to fall, but about patiently erasing all the layers that have brought us here. It's a slow process."

"It didn't take the French that long. Of course, they used guillotines."

Najwa brought her hands to her face and grumbled.

"Dude, don't you ever get tired? Aren't you sleepy?"

No. I'm not tired, I thought.

In fact, I feel like running.

14

RAMOS IS A DOCTOR. An ophthalmologist. He defines himself as progressive, even though he votes either center-left or center-right, depending on which way the winds are blowing. Garbo and Hugo call him "Ramos" because almost every time they see him he is carrying an enormous, bright, colorful bouquet of flowers—a *ramo*—in one hand. He doesn't mind the nickname.

"Yesterday I went too far with her," he says.

Ramos is a serial psychological abuser. He says he's never laid a hand on his wife, and they believe him, because he's as thin as a razor blade and doesn't seem prone to physical effort. He gets tired easily, he has asthma, he only goes into bars where he can sit down. When he returns from the bathroom or the bar, he's out of breath. Especially if he's carrying a couple of pints. He has chronic pain in his back, and in his left wrist, in his neck, and on the soles of his feet. Like all men of short stature, he has a very bad temperament.

"If it weren't for the kids, I'd kick that whore to the curb. To do the only thing she knows how to do."

Despite the fact that his wife is an elementary school teacher who volunteers at an old-age home on weekends while her children are at tennis class, to hear Ramos tell it she's a man-eater who lives to offer herself up to any man she happens upon. He employs so many adjectives to refer to her that we almost dubbed him "Thesaurus," but it didn't exactly roll off the tongue the way "Ramos" does. He controls her cell phone and laptop, checks her Facebook status every fifteen minutes; he knows who calls her and sends her messages and whom she writes to, but when she's the one who calls him for some reason, he explodes with rage, accusing her of being controlling, obsessive, and hysterical before hanging up on her. Or even worse, he'll respond, saying "What the fuck do you want? I told you I'm having a drink with my friends. Isn't there someone you can give an STD to somewhere? Fuck off."

Garbo and Hugo noticed him early one evening at an outdoor table, when he started to lay into a waitress who'd made a mistake with his change.

"Useless whore" and "Stay home if you're on the rag" and "Go back to the kitchen, thief" were some of the phrases with which he expressed his displeasure, as the rest of the customers stared in shock while trying to pretend they hadn't heard a thing. The waitress couldn't have been older than nineteen. Ramos yelled so much that the manager had to come over to ask him to leave, but he stood his ground and refused to be cowed by what was, clearly, a horrific affront to his personage, so he kept screaming until he managed to get them to bring over the complaints book and a plate of olives "for the inconvenience." He ate the olives one by one, very slowly, and every time the waitress passed by on her way to another table, he would murmur, "Man, if I were your father..."

He most definitely had the proper attitude to join the group.

They followed him to the next bar, and there they struck up a conversation with him, showing enthusiasm for his behavior at the previous place, congratulating him for his virile unflappability, his forcefulness, and his sense of justice. Ramos lasted five minutes on his feet, humbly appreciating their flattery, before inviting them to sit down together at a free table. A few hours later, he was already totally convinced that it was necessary to take sides to keep women from turning the modern world into a schoolyard covered with used tampons and condoms. Just like his bitch of a wife probably did, when she was alone, with the toilet bowl.

He was the one who introduced them to Aguirre, one of his clients.

Aguirre is bothered by the language Hugo and Ramos use when referring to women: too many curse words and offensive epithets, unbefitting—in his opinion—upright men. He is an archetype of jesuitical discipline, thin as a Christ figure, tolerant, conservative, and always restrained in his speech. Early to bed and early to rise, like the good literature professor he is. He keeps extra eyeglasses in his trench coat and in his car, in addition to the pairs spread throughout his house and his country home, just in case. He loves cognac, thin cigars, and the Spanish Golden Age.

"If you'll allow me, I'd like to qualify what I said earlier..." he often says.

His manners can be exasperating.

He doesn't share all of the rest of the group's ideas, and obviously is even less in favor of their methods. For him women are goddesses of fertility and must be treated as such: as women are wombs where the male seed will grow, it is the work of all men to protect them, take care of them, and not allow them to depart from their "sacred mandate" [*sic*], which includes keeping them from eminently masculine vices such as alcohol, tobacco, and gambling, and refusing them access to the work market, a setting for which their aptitudes have proved insufficiently developed and where—which is worse—they tend to forget, out of distraction or inertia, their true place in the world. Which is, of course, none other than at home, taking care of the children.

Garbo was about to eliminate him from the list because he seemed unprepared, but Aguirre has a weak point: feminists. He completely loses his mind when they enter the equation. His phobia toward what he calls "the anti-women" is so visceral that it becomes a caricature of itself, and fluctuates between the unblemished behavior of a seminary student and the incendiary babbling of a hooligan high on coke, like a comic representation of Dr. Jekyll and his private monster. Every feminist demand incites him: free access to abortion, quotas, wage equity, inclusive language. He's suspicious of every woman with short hair or baggy clothes, except when they are recovering from cancer or in an advanced gestational state, situations he somewhat begrudgingly accepts. He feels a ferociously virulent disgust for female body hair. When he goes too far, threatening burning at the stake or torture on the racks for some woman protesting for her rights, he immediately grows ashamed for overstepping his moral limits, and apologizes to his mates.

"I shouldn't have said that...I'm sorry. But she deserved it."

That was why Aguirre is part of the group: Garbo thinks he gives a special balance to his small army.

Hugo believes it's the moment to begin to act. To do things. His first proposal is solid: reviewing social media, going to the first scheduled women's demonstration, and dumping white paint on them.

"As if it were semen," he says.

In general, his idea is convincing. Garbo speaks next, and they all listen, because he is the mastermind, and as such, the spiritual leader of their crusade.

"We have a lot of work ahead of us, but it is important that you remember something. That you brand this into your mind: we must be invisible. Anonymous. Faceless. We cannot allow them to recognize us."

"Why?" asks Ramos. "I have nothing to hide."

"I know. Me either. But society is hypocritical, and the authorities have caved to all these fucking women's petty demands."

"Language..." whispers Aguirre.

"We all have jobs we depend on to support ourselves, and a family, and a social life outside of this group. Even though our cause is as valid as any other, for the moment we have to act in the shadows. We don't want to endanger our physical integrity, or our wages, or our clientele. We don't want the enemy to name us and harass our loved ones. When there are more of us, when we are sure we have the support of an indisputable number of men and our actions are endorsed by that silent majority, that's when we'll be able to show our faces. Until then, shadows."

The group concedes his point.

"And what do you suggest as a starting point?" asks Hugo.

"Heating things up. Make fake profiles for yourselves on all the social networks. Hang up anonymous signs in your doorways, at your workplaces, in business entrances, by night. Buy burner phones at the dollar store and send out our message. Write letters with random names to newspapers and radio stations. Do whatever you can to promote our goal: reminding women just who's in charge. I want them to feel humiliated. I want them desperate and anxious. I want them to burn like matches, angry, hysterical. And then for them to bow their heads and go back home crying, the way they always do. Because that's all they know how to do."

His epic tone works. Garbo receives a round of applause.

"And one more thing," he says. "Look at us. Take a good look: we don't have warrior physiques.

Let's be realistic, we're below average. If we want to carry out impressive actions, unforgettable ones, we need muscle. Find some."

"Suck on this muscle I got between my legs," says Hugo.

Garbo breathes like a conspirator.

15

MY MOTHER went on vacation.

Well, not exactly. She went for a weekend away with some girlfriends, from Friday to Sunday, two nights. Fifty kilometers from her house. But to hear her describe it, it's a vacation. She told me she wanted a break from the fisherman, from my cousin's kid, from everybody; she said she needed some breathing room, and not to call until Monday.

I didn't even know my mother had girlfriends.

Najwa was also out of town. She needs to beef up her résumé so she can apply for a university position and she's taking part in a five-day conference in Lisbon, all paid for out of her own pocket: travel expenses, hotel, food and drink. Knowing her, she probably ate a Spartan diet based on carbs so she could spend the rest of her budget on decent wine, and bolster her agenda. The academic world never ceases to amaze me.

I'm still out of work. I've given up for dead the man I once was, and now devote myself entirely to my new labors.

Conclusion: I turned the apartment into a safe house.

On one hand, there's the computer equipment: an old laptop, the burner cell, and a tablet. With them I control everything the group members are doing online, and I implement new areas of action. Apart from my Twitter pseudonym, I've created more than a hundred new identities that are tied to each other through Facebook, LinkedIn, and other social networks I'm not even familiar with, but that young people use. Hugo explained how we can do it without being detected by a regular user. I keep a detailed, password-protected Excel spreadsheet of each of these identities, because I am extremely active and don't want to get them mixed-up.

On the other hand are the production props: signage, balloons, duct tape, rope, zip ties, a towel, a bucket, an expandable baton, two flashlights, a huge black dildo, markers, sleeping pills, a flag-pole, three dozen eggs, a Palestinian scarf, con-doms, old underwear, shoe polish, a flask, various thirty-three-centiliter glass bottles, a white sheet, a Swiss Army knife, industrial oil, marbles, a nail gun, gloves, headphones, a carabiner, hand cream, a small megaphone, two grams of MDMA, a box of rubber bands, prepaid envelopes, various lighters, four black T-shirts, the license plates off my grandfather's old Renault, a Bluetooth speaker, ibuprofen, aspirin, Band-Aids. My part of the supplies.

On the ground is a three-by-two-meter map of the city.

Blue thumbtacks: the places where we usually meet up.

Black thumbtacks: the places where we live.

Green thumbtacks: the places where we work.

Red thumbtacks: the places where there are usually feminist demonstrations.

Purple thumbtacks: women-only bars.

White thumbtacks: specific targets.

I've marked in red the main avenues, police stations, and the streets around them. In green, the best escape routes if chased. I've divided the map into quadrants and photographed them, one by one. In the margins I've written the dates of the upcoming gatherings, organized by groups that defend women's rights.

I'm exhausted.

I get up and look around: the living room looks like the garage of an amateur terrorist, or a hyperactive child.

If Najwa were to return without warning and find me like this, surrounded by tools and papers and electronic devices, I would be incapable of coming up with a solid excuse that would explain my motives. Most likely she would quickly realize my intentions: her specialty is textual analysis, and everything is text—as she would say—everything from the Palestinian scarf to the color of the thumbtacks, from the glass bottles to the Swiss Army knife. Would it be the end of our relationship? Should I be honest with her?

I grab a piece of paper and write a series of responses that could buy me some time and serve as an alibi:

Trivial: "I was trying to organize my stuff."

Severe: "Don't distract me now, I'll explain it
    to you tomorrow."

Curt: "It's personal."

Elegant: "Good question, but it's not the best
    moment to explain."

Offended: "I have a right to my privacy."

Sneaky: "Don't look, it's a surprise for your
    birthday."

Odd: "I've gotten hooked on role-playing
    games."

Vicious: "You're looking for trouble."

For some reason I'm still not sure how to put into words, because I sense a discrepancy in my discourse but I'm unable to put my finger on it, when I write the word *honest*, I end up leaving the rest of the page blank.

16

EXCEPT FOR THE FACT that Aguirre considers homosexuality an illness that requires clinical treatment with therapy or pills, like a bad flu that can be cured if the patient does his or her part, and the fact that Bruno is gay, the group is functioning in complete harmony and productivity.

Aguirre insists that some man must have infected Bruno, that no one is born homosexual. "The Carrier," he calls this man.

Luckily, Bruno's size and girth forces him to be prudent and not just use his strength against people like Aguirre, or against any of them, because he'd probably end up in prison for attempted homicide. It's a question of honor. The only one who can compete with him is Donovan, who in addition to being at least as buff as Bruno, is a Krav Maga teacher.

Nobody knows what gym Hugo found them at.

Bruno and Donovan have been friends for years, both big as hippos and both woman haters. The former is misogynistic by nature: from his perspective, heterosexuality is not only an aberration, but a demonstration of how much weak men like to wallow in filth, like pigs. Women are a subspecies of the human genre. The latter is a misogynist out of spite: every girlfriend he's ever had has dumped him, most of them choosing a mutual friend or colleague over him. His insecurity led him to assume that he would find love if he increased the size of his biceps, triceps, and pecs, if he learned to kill with his bare hands and if he transformed himself into an archetype of the macho man: brave and hard. His transformation didn't change his relationship status, and that cut him to the quick. He probably holds the world record for using the word *bitch* most often.

"They're all bitches, take it from me," he eventually announces.

The others nod, slightly amused by the contrast between his little-boy voice, tinged with a strong Latin American accent, and his size.

"Bitches, total bitches."

Aguirre has stopped complaining. Now he covers his ears.

The last few days have been hectic. The cyber-activity of everyone in the group, especially Hugo and Garbo, has obtained unexpected results: thousands of followers; several reports for harassment, incitement to violence, or defending sexist violence; three accounts blocked ad infinitum and another few warned; repercussions on blogs and some media outlets that specialize in gender issues. An unprecedented success, in barely a month. They'd made even bigger inroads in the analog world: the signs and phone calls caused a big stir, especially when they'd targeted family planning centers and book clubs for women's lit. Some women made reports to the police, who sheepishly took down their complaints, and others showed their condemnation on Facebook and Twitter, with considerable societal echoes. When the group members returned to the scenes of their crimes to study the scope of their actions, they saw tears, hysteria, and in some cases, rage. The discreetly taken photographs, seasoned with jokey comments and uploaded on one of the fake accounts, went viral among many men who share the group's ideas, certain sports journalists, and some extreme right-wing politicians.

Today was a special day: the first big, elaborate operation.

The objective was sabotaging a conference on "The Space of Feminism in the 21st Century" that was hours away from starting. After intense debate,

Garbo and the others organized the following program of activities:

1. Blocking the entrance door
2. A little gift for each of the participants
3. A welcome sign in the middle of the main table
4. Exclusive decorations
5. Pleasant atmosphere

Sealing the lock to the function room with silicone was the easiest part, and the final one. The rest of the program cost time and money, but the group's determination won out over petty bickering. Bruno oversaw the decorating: tons of medium-format photographs of giant penises, women kneeling on the ground, and scenes of sexual violence. No one wanted to be in charge of the pen drive that held the material, much less go to the copy shop to print it out, but he had a former colleague who was now a freelancer and had the necessary tools. It wasn't cheap, especially with the bonus for his discretion, but it was worth it. Ramos and Aguirre prepared the gift bags, which each held a safety razor, a lipstick, and some fishnet stockings. There were a total of one hundred and fifty bags. There was some discussion about how to divide up the shopping logistically in terms of distance and time: no one wanted to show up in a beauty supply store and buy everything at once. Besides that, neither Ramos nor Aguirre were willing to store them in their homes for the days prior to the event, because their wives could draw the wrong conclusions. It was suggested that Bruno hold on to them.

"Not on your life. The first time I saw a pussy I knew I was gay. Pussies are probably, along with snails, the most repulsive creations in nature. A shapeless, damp, smelly hole. They have all kinds of weird elastic folds, like a piece of gum that's been in several people's mouths. They smell like a port in the evening, when the cats go there to eat. I don't like gum, or cats. I don't even want to get close to a feminine beauty product. Is that clear?"

In the end, they agreed to use the trunk of Donovan's car. He was the one in charge of the atmosphere: when the speakers and participants managed to get into the room, after an hour of waiting and a last-minute locksmith, when they'd recovered from the impact of the images and the gifts, when they'd ripped off the welcome sign, and when, finally, the organizers had presented the conferences and opened up the debate, Donovan took advantage of the darkness—he sat down in one of the back rows and let two dozen stink bombs roll through the entire space.

According to his calculations, the conference lasted nine minutes before being definitively canceled.

Without a doubt the most problematic aspect was the composing of the welcome sign, a small tribute to the flyers thrown by the feminists at the 1970 Miss World pageant. It was somehow the group's first public manifesto, and as such it needed a signature.

The final text, so to speak, was a documentation of the deliberations, and was not unanimously approved.

17

WELCOME, FEMINIST WHORES:

It's a pleasure for us to not be here listening to your shrill voices spouting nonsense,
not to see your neglected bodies, not to smell
your estrogen or your panties lined with
maxi-pads. We hope you won't leave pools
of blood on the seats, so you don't infect the
next child who sits in them.

Regardless, we have some gift bags for
you (presumably you'll know how to use
them with the proper instructions), and some
warnings/recommendations for how we can
all get along in the future:

You are not beautiful, you're ugly.

You'll always be beneath men.

The feminist struggle is an invention of nymphomaniac lesbians.

You all dream of a good cock.

Shave: your moustaches and the hair in your armpits is really gross.

A woman without makeup is like any other herbivore.

Release your inner whore.

Keep bowing your heads, especially between our legs.

You always deserve a good smack.

Appreciatively,
PHALLIC STATE

18

MY FRIENDS' CHILDREN are the revolutionary tax of friendship.

Every once in a while, we all get together on a pedestrian street so their kids can run wild, and we can keep an eye on them while we have some wine and talk about adult stuff. Always in the late morning, before lunch. It's one of the few occasions when I can also be with my female friends, and hold a conversation that lasts more than five minutes without interruptions.

I like kids. I like them enough to consider having a few some day, especially with Najwa: I think we could be good at it. But I'm able to recognize the tedium involved, at least at these ages, with trying to combine them with a social life. The oldest is five, and it's easy to lose sight of him. Even I get panicked, without meaning to, in the middle of a sentence, when I can't find him on the horizon. I wonder if the protection instinct is contagious.

I get into a lot of heated discussions about parenthood and child-rearing, especially with the women.

@feminassti
I'm going to rent out your testicles, macho man.
Then you'll understand.

They are intelligent, modern people, who don't just allow themselves to be carried along by the inertia with which they were raised. They talk to me about breastfeeding and maternity leave, so they can be with their children during their first year of life, of shorter working days, of the expense of diapers, clothes, and gifts. I take it all in, like I'm studying for a master's. They bring up thought-provoking topics, backed up by statistics: schooling ages, appropriate readings, teaching models, nutrition, entertainment. Since I'm so wrapped up in my obsessions, I ask them about time distribution: it's clear the fathers go out more; therefore they drink more; therefore they have more escape valves, so to speak.

"It's temporary," says one of my female friends. "The first few years, with the nursing and maternity leave, it's logical that the kids spend more time with us and the men can go out more often."

I ask if the intensity of child-rearing will have consequences for them later on, because they have so little space to vent, and I question whether they'll be able to make up that lost time, to which they respond that it isn't lost time, but time invested in other activities. I'm convinced by the argument. Then I focus on theoretical gender discrimination: blue or pink clothes? Balls for boys, dolls for girls? Superheroes and princesses?

As I said, they're modern people. They opt for freedom of choice and common sense—in other words, they let the kids choose according to their preferences and needs, without historical prejudices, and allow them to learn from their social environs, even though that generally involves reproducing behavioral patterns that segregate by gender. As parents, they are careful not to legitimize hierarchical conduct, and promote egalitarian coexistence both in public and private, so the next generation doesn't inherit the vices of the previous ones, at least through their family.

Every parent these days is a pedagogue.

Their discourse is perfect, but I can't help noticing that the boys are playing soccer—with an older girl I don't know, that's true—and that the girls are clustered around a talking doll. Assuming that there are exceptions, I point that out. I tell them about a thesis Najwa explained to me about the capitalization of some public children's spaces: most school playgrounds are filled with a soccer field, with its lines and goal areas, so that those kids who don't want to play are relegated to the margins of that field, to the corners; so those girls who prefer not to kick around a ball during recess accept, unconsciously, that the center of the available public space belongs to the boys, since they are the ones—generally—who play soccer. I try to express my skepticism. It doesn't seem worth the effort. I mean: if society is built on these binary parameters, and since the individual—except for the anomalies—ends up ceding autonomy in favor of integration, is there any point to raising children for a world that doesn't exist, or that will cease to exist when they turn six, seven, eight years old? I have the impression that no matter what they do, they won't be able to avoid their sons being potential sexists, and their daughters being stoic submissives. Personal experience and the collective imagination will decide for them.

Maybe I came into this world to argue, and I enjoy it, but there is something about what I've just done that doesn't sit well with me: I used a previous conversation with Najwa as the basis of my argument. I can almost smell the cologne my father and my uncles wear. Did I purposely leave out the fact that it was my girlfriend who told me that story?

Before coming to any conclusion, I realize I've struck a nerve. After my words, no one can agree on anything. I become the devil's advocate.

"My son will never be abusive."

Until some girl tells him she likes bad boys.

"Complete equality will come in the future."

In four centuries. Not even your grandkids will see it.

"I'll teach my daughter not to resign herself."

Because if she were a man you wouldn't have to.

"The world is evolving."

And devolving, with every war. The heroes are always men.

"We need to have patience."

That's it: quiet and patient. We wouldn't want to interrupt the routine of the forces that put us each in our place.

"Society can't be changed from one day to the next."

Tell that to Osama bin Laden.

Somehow, I manage to get everybody pissed off. Mostly at me, but also at each other. I'm a terrible conversationalist, because I interrupt all the time and don't listen, like I was a parent myself. I sense that it's time for me to vanish without hugs or goodbyes, while no one's looking. But I have one last question.

"And what if your daughter told you that she wants to be a boy, or vice versa? What would you do?"

I've touched a nerve, so hard I think I broke it. They rush to speak, all at the same time. People stare because we're getting louder. One of the children listens to us attentively, from below, barely a couple of centimeters from my knees. He's so small that I'm embarrassed about what I've started, because his world is as small as he is. I tell them that I'll be right back, but it's a lie. I take a ridiculously circuitous route so they don't see me, and I leave, my head swollen with doubts. I see them arguing as I head off.

I need to talk to Najwa. And that feeling is beginning to bother me, because Najwa isn't my therapist, or my professor, or my mother. Am I actually incapable of forming my own opinion without appropriating hers? Why think when I have her? Why read when she tells me about what she's reading? Why invite her along with my friends when I can substitute her with a few sentences, some headlines, the entertaining repetition of our conversations. Am I making Najwa disappear?

No, I'm not that kind of a man. I refuse to believe that.

I'm the most feminist guy in the world. Najwa and I love each other, we share everything. Even words.

We have a level playing field.

This phrase, however, doesn't echo in my head like an affirmation.

19

WHITE THUMBTACKS.

In one of the first Phallic State meetings, each member chose a specific target. They didn't have to explain: it was enough to jot down the name, and the rest of the group assumed they had their reasons. It was an exercise in solidarity and trust that Garbo didn't agree with, because acting against particular women went against the globalizing purpose of his ideology and didn't involve yields beyond the personal, but the majority won out: if they were going to break the law, they all should know how committed they each were to the group, as a guarantee. A blood pact.

During recent weeks the group had exponentially increased their actions, torpedoing several feminist events, dampening the participation in dozens of gatherings, humiliating protestors and activists, stealing materials, dirtying stages, threatening small groups with violence, drugging speakers. Someone had created a support website, and it wasn't any of the members. They have more followers every day. In other cities there are copycats carrying out similar actions, under the same name. Women's organizations, on the other hand, except for the traditional declarations of censure, haven't reacted.

Garbo wants to take a step forward, but first he must attend to the demands of his group and fulfill old commitments: the white thumbtacks.

In order to make the process ceremonious, they assign the names of six of the nine classic muses to the women they plan to attack, like military code. Symbolically, it has a certain coherence to it. Aguirre is given Polyhymnia, muse of sacred poetry; Ramos, Thalia, muse of comedy; Donovan, Melpomene, muse of tragedy; Hugo, Clio, muse of history; Bruno, Euterpe, muse of music; and Garbo, Calliope, muse of beauty and epic poetry.

Polyhymnia is a young college student who usually demonstrates with her herd of radical feminists in front of the church where Aguirre volunteers on Sundays. Their motives are varied, sometimes for and sometimes against: the right to abortion, female popes, nuns who steal kids, pedophile priests.

There's a different cause each month. Aguirre would like to crucify her, literally. With nails. Instead, they convince him that ruining her professional career would be a victory.

Strategy: photoshopped pictures on social media, calls to the dean from groups defending family values, insinuations of the consumption and trafficking of cocaine in the family environment, prostitutes reporting harassment and abuse, telephone stalking, threats, graffiti on her house.

Result: depression, dropping out of college, moving back to her hometown.

Thalia is the best friend of Ramos's wife. He's convinced she acts as an intermediary between his wife and an incalculable number of sporadic lovers, as well as being the protagonist of some lesbian episodes he'd rather not confirm. She's about fifty years old and works at the post office. Like every other bitch like her, in Ramos's words, she has no partner or kids.

Strategy: daily complaints to her workplace for alcoholism and laziness, destruction of her personal vehicle, constant theft of her mail cart.

Result: losing her job, eviction.

Melpomene is a cocktail waitress at a hip bar. She has the figure of a lingerie model and the attitude of the French prime minister when the conservatives are in power. She went out with Donovan three times: the first time, she let him kiss her good-night; the second, she went up to his place, laughed at the size of his penis and left him there naked; the third time, she demanded he not ever come back into the bar. Even though he can't admit it, it is clear that Donovan is still in love with her.

Strategy: rumors of venereal diseases, warning her current partner of her infidelity, raising suspicions that she is pocketing cash at work.

Result: dismissal, breakup, poor nutrition, dark circles under the eyes, two sizes up at her next shopping trip.

Clio is one of Hugo's coworkers. Asian, upper-class, svelte. She spread the rumor that he was a priapic, harassing pig obsessed with the female body and got the rest of the women in their department to stop talking to him, so he has to eat alone or with junior associates. Hugo usually masturbates thinking of her, imagining a gangbang with fisting, anal, and bukkake. In any case, he doesn't want her to leave the office.

Strategy: anonymous threats of rape, squirting syringes full of semen onto her clothes and hair on mass transit, chauvinistic leafleting.

Result: laughs.

Euterpe is Bruno's natural enemy: lesbian, misandrist, an exercise addict and an extrovert. She worked for a while at his gym, they had a few run-ins, and ever since then they've hated each other. They occasionally see each other at CrossFit events and fun runs. He only socializes with men, and she with women. The way he describes it, it sounds like a duel between rival street gangs, and that's why he only would accept a strategy based on physical pain, which raises a number of red flags. Psychological harm is more lasting, they protest. In the end, they come to a compromise.

Strategy: tampering with her mountain bike.

Result: knee injury, meniscus surgery, six months of recovery, with no sports allowed.

Calliope is Garbo's muse.

He doesn't want to give too many details about her, which rubs some of the group's members the wrong way. He says he doesn't know where she lives, but that it doesn't matter. She is a specialist in feminism at the university, petite and with glasses, who may have taken part in some of the acts they've sabotaged; she's very active on social networks and certain media outlets, bellicose, pro-animal rights, ecologist, atheist. The full package.

"We'll use a different strategy with her," says Garbo.

The group listens, oblivious to the fact that their leader is about to vomit.

20

NAJWA IS FURIOUS when she gets home, but she doesn't want me to notice.

She barely looks into my eyes when she speaks: instead she looks at my chin, or my chest, or a point a few centimeters from my head. She isn't a particularly smiley person, but around me her dimples show up when she's happy and feeling relaxed. Today she has no dimples. She is moving around robotically, brusquely, carelessly, opening and closing cabinets noisily, leaving the lights on when she exits a room.

As long as she doesn't tell me what's going on, I'll pretend I haven't noticed.

On days like this, it's not easy to talk to her, because her tone of voice has little variation or nuance and it's impossible to know whether her response is aggressive because of the question itself or if it is simply a product of her bad mood. The best thing is to give her space, like she does with me every morning until my coffee kicks in, waiting for me to be the one to start the conversation. I pretend to be distracted with my cell phone.

@feminassti
In an ideal world, aborting boy babies should be legal up until the day of delivery.

Najwa sits down in front of me, looks at her phone for a little while, retweets something by @feminassti, and then puts her phone down on the table. She's just washed her face; there are still drops of water on her eyelashes. She is serious, nervous. Her eyes are bloodshot, as if she'd been scratching them.

I know what I shouldn't say.

"How was your week?" she asks me. "I've been swamped since I got back from Lisbon, and we've hardly seen each other. Did you get together with your friends in the end?"

She is making an effort to sound friendly. I pick up the gauntlet.

"Yes. I wanted to talk to you about that."

"Why? Did something happen?"

"Well, there was a near argument, you could say..."

"What'd you do this time?"

I light a cigarette.

"I swear, I don't know how it happened," I laugh.

"Yeah. Sure."

"I started asking them about how they are raising their kids, and one thing led to another. I asked them about gender differences and how to resolve the conflict between what's taught at home and what happens out in the world...the real world."

"Again?"

"I couldn't help myself."

"I think you're too obsessed with the subject. Besides, it's not your subject."

It's not? How could it not be? I erase her last comment from my memory, as if it were unimportant. I try to continue with the debate.

"Perhaps. But I put forth an interesting question. I wanted to know your opinion."

"Go ahead."

"If your son tells you, I don't know, at four years old, that he doesn't want to be a boy, that he feels like a girl, what do you do?"

Najwa straightens up and moves her head to either side, drawing circles. I hear her neck crack, five, six times. It gives me shivers, but I know where it comes from. I imagine her suffering my group's attacks every day, at the university, in the cafeteria, in bar bathrooms, just the way I planned it. I imagine her entering a loop of rage that now, in front of me, she struggles to restrain.

"Oof, that," she says.

Her voice is dry.

"Forget about it. It was just hypothetical. Let's watch some TV."

"No, no. I'll answer you. You know what I think about gender: it's nurture, not nature. The biological differences don't define our gender, because it's an ideological construct, a social inheritance."

"I know. That's why you believe in a future without..."

"Don't interrupt. Yes: I believe in a future without gender, or without binary gender. Which would surely be a utopia. But if I'm coherent with that reasoning, if I assume that genitalia mean absolutely nothing, what that boy has is a discourse disease. A contamination."

"What?"

"I know! It sounds terrible. He's just a kid! And I would never say it in public, but I'm fed up. I've fucking had it up to here!"

Her eyes are very wide and her hands are tense. I don't think she's talking to me. She's received a total of fifty messages, between letters to her office, notes on the blackboard, comments made by anonymous men in the street, and graffiti. We have lynched her by millimeters.

"Had it up to here with what?"

"Look: that boy isn't happy with his body, with his dick, because the world around him has told him that *dick* means a certain way of behaving. It's just the same as people who get cosmetic surgery because they're dissatisfied. Since they don't fit into the beauty canon of their times, they mutilate themselves. Happiness through amputation, through abuse of their bodies. Through modifying their flesh. What the fuck do you want me to say to that kid? That I think it's a good idea for him to cut off his balls and get a cunt? That a good hole will change everything?"

"Shit, Najwa, we're not living in a future without binaries. Trans…"

"That's the fucking problem! Transsexuals, faggots, dykes, all those fucking minorities are occupying the media space, and the public accepts their discourse. Because it's fashionable. Because we should protect their rights. For fuck's sake: women should occupy that space, even just out of seniority. Aren't there more women than gay men, for fuck's sake? Is some fucking millionaire architect going to tell me that he's very put out because he likes to suck cock and they won't let him buy a uterus? Really?"

She says things she doesn't mean, or she doesn't want to think. She's overacting. She blushes. Her hands and knees tremble. In my head a red pilot light goes on, trying to warn me to stop: not the conversation, but all the other stuff. I ignore it.

"One struggle doesn't invalidate the other," I say.

She looks at me sadly.

"You're right. That is the dark flip side of collectivizing. It's like with nation-states. When you accept forming part of a group, you exclude all the others. Either I'm a radical nationalist, or I'm a utopian humanist who doesn't take sides, but I can't be both. Even though I know I should aspire to some compromise. Human beings suck..."

She received the last message a couple of hours ago. In a bar. Aguirre was watching her. When she went into the bathroom and lifted the toilet lid, she found, again, written on a piece of paper, the phrase we've been using to harass her for days now.

You should smile more, pretty lady.

It might seem trivial, but I know that symbolism affects Najwa deeply. She cannot stand what feminine kindness means, how it's the price to pay for being lovable. She thinks women who smile all the time are like lobotomized mares.

Her kidneys must still be hurting her.

According to Aguirre, she slammed down the toilet lid so hard it broke. One of the waiters heard her yelling and tried to calm her. She was out of control: she checked under every stall door, and when she saw the other messages, she started kicking all the stalls. They threw her out of the bar.

I tell her that I'm going to bed, that I want to get up early, that we'll continue talking some other day. She apologizes for her intensity.

"I love your intensity," I tell her.

She smiles at me. A little smile, but still.

Now I really know what I shouldn't say, under any circumstances.

With all the love I'm capable of showing in a gesture, in my tone of voice, in my way of looking at the woman I love, I stand up, kiss her on the forehead and whisper:

"I love it when you smile."

She doesn't respond. She sits there, alone, still, in silence, like a corpse.

21

PHALLIC STATE has an adversary.

It doesn't seem to be as solid of a group, but it's very large and very active. Its appearance has provoked an emergency meeting at Hugo's house.

"They're such pussies," he jokes.

It began as an online platform to support the feminist collectives that Garbo and his group were attacking. It quickly went viral and gained all sorts of support, moving from passive resistance to direct action, and from the cyberworld to the physical one. Until yesterday, the new group's biggest achievement was guaranteeing the proper functioning of a series of roundtables and conferences, protecting the centers where they were scheduled, with groups guarding them in eight-hour shifts, starting the day before, with surveillance protocols at the entrances.

Of course, Phallic State was thwarted from acting: there were women everywhere.

However, last night the group moved to direct attack.

It was a premeditated assault on several fronts. They hacked the websites and a large number of the fake identities that the group was using to promote itself on social media networks. Throughout the Internet, they planted offensive videos against the patriarchy, feminist jokes, calls to revolution, and death threats against Phallic State. They drew penises inside bull's-eyes on almost every street in the center of the city. Various squads, holding torches, their identities protected by burnt Disney Princess masks, threw stained tampons from cars at people standing in line to get into various fashionable bars. According to reports of those affected, the tampons were not stained with paint. Finally, the group published a manifesto declaring war on the heteropatriarchal system, warning of its ability to operate in various cities at the same time and demanding an unconditional general surrender to avoid an escalation of violence. The surrender or support should be demonstrated by flags or light-colored sheets with the letter W—for Women—and the letter M—for Mujeres—written in red. As a signature, the banners should read: "We take back the night and the day."

"They're all talk and no trousers," says Donovan. "On Saturday they'll be too busy putting on makeup and they'll have forgotten all about us. I know women: they heat up quickly, but then they cool down."

Garbo wasn't so sure.

"And what if they're serious?"

"What do you mean by 'serious'?" asks Ramos. "Are they going to beat us up? Kill us? Ooh, I'm scared. Shaking in my boots. A bunch of bitches armed with tampons and nail polish, the army of darkness."

"I can take out four of them with one blow," says Bruno.

Aguirre doesn't interject. Garbo calls him out. "What do you think?"

The altar boy takes off his glasses, cleans them with a handkerchief, and puts them back on, slowly.

"I think they are servants of Satan."

Murmuring. Complaints. Hugo makes the sign of the cross. Aguirre keeps talking.

"Our actions have not been those of just men. We've lied, robbed, insulted, and humiliated, going against God's laws. It is true that we've done it for a noble cause, in accordance with the divine word, and that soldiers are forced to make difficult decisions, when the ends justify them."

"Shit, you're not in mass," interrupts Bruno.

"But everything we do in life has consequences. And the consequence of our actions has been to open the gates of hell. Don't look at me like that. When man picks up the devil's tools, the devil comes looking for them. We called him. We amplified his voice. This is his way of answering us."

Despite his one-note homily tone, his words puncture the confidence of the other group members, who stop laughing and making fun of him. Because his speech reveals a truth that the other five hadn't been counting on: that sooner or later the women would stand up to them.

Garbo smiles.

"So, what should we do? Go after them or ignore them?"

"Are they mobilizing others?" asks Ramos.

Hugo does a search on his phone. Then he gets up, opens the window and sticks his head out, looking right and left.

"Not really. In Twitter they're posting photos of balconies with the famous flag, which is actually just a shitty painted rag. A hundred, hundred and twenty. If they're calling the whole country to action, it's a slow start. I haven't seen any in this neighborhood. I don't think."

"Then let's fucking ignore them."

Garbo's open hand is the focal point of everyone's gaze.

"What if not doing anything is taken as a sign of weakness? Maybe today there are only a hundred flags, but where do we draw the line? Five hundred? A thousand? I'm sure they aren't going to stop, or get bored, or quit sabotaging our actions: what happened last night was organized. They are imitating the activists from the late seventies. Maybe it's better to take charge now, when they're still getting started, instead of waiting for them to multiply. Remember that women, when they want to, really band together."

"And who do we take charge against?" says Ramos. "We don't even know who they are! They don't even have names. It could be any gang of bitches we pass on the street. Except if we catch them with those masks on."

"We need to give them a name," says Donovan.

"The Cunts!" shouts Hugo.

Some alternatives are bandied about: the Superhos, the Holes, Rent-a-Wombs, Divine Treasure. The hard dialectics last through several liters of beer and two bottles of wine, but in the end they agree to take firm measures against them and adopt the name suggested by Garbo.

The Princesses.

Surely they'll appreciate the homage.

22

THE COEXISTENCE FALLACY is me and Najwa pretending that absolutely nothing is going on, that the days are slipping by peacefully, that I'm busy with my small-time journalistic stuff and that she's working on her thesis, researching, preparing classes. What do you want for dinner, I did the shopping, I like the way your beard looks, why don't we go for a walk.

There's no doubt about it: this is the cold war.

I started to think that a while ago, when the actions of Phallic State started to have such a large impact, that it was absurd—given our fondness for talking about everything and especially about everything related to gender studies—that neither of us had brought it up. Maybe it was a mistake on my part, but I never found a way to discuss the subject without revealing my active participation: as I always say, she is very good at analyzing texts, and I am a text myself, probably one of the simplest she's come across. Once I'd accepted my error, there were four possible options for interpreting her uncomfortable silence:

1. That she hadn't realized what we were doing.
2. That she'd been traumatized by our direct attack on her.
3. That she suspected I was behind everything.
4. That she had her own plan.

I ruled out the first one, because I knew for certain that we had sabotaged some events that she was planning on attending. I then ruled out the second one, because her personality hadn't lost even a hint of its strength, and I hadn't seen her defeated when stating her opinions; quite the opposite, she seemed to have hardened, like a noble soldier who loses his decency on his first tour, and can't sleep, and hears a constant buzzing in his ears. The third one was still possible, of course, but I'd been extremely careful, and I doubted, to the extent my conscience allowed, that some misstep on my part or some premonition on hers would have driven her to violate the privacy of my electronic devices or my email. That left only one possibility.

"This ceviche you made is fantastic," she says.

My suspicions grew over the last few days, when we responded to the demonstration by the Princesses and their spontaneous attacks with our typical restraint: we painted over all their graffiti with enormous, smiling hairy penises, we published videos of their flag in flames, edited to include Disney soundtrack songs so they seemed more childish and less aggressive, and we cleverly chose smaller events to thwart, ones that weren't protected by their collaborators. In less than a day they'd deemed us "the militant branch of the enemy" and challenged all women to seek us out and beat us up. Not in those words: "We summon you to take the necessary measures to halt the activities of this group of fanatics." We remained firm, although we increased our security measures and were more careful, just in case. The social networks and some media outlets began to take what was happening more seriously, with articles and feature stories, but at home a ridiculously saccharine peace reigned, worthy of better players.

"The corvina was incredibly fresh," I replied.

I accepted my analysis as definitive: the only reason Najwa hadn't mentioned the Princesses even once must be the same reason I had never once mentioned Phallic State. We were both in it up to our eyeballs. It's only logical.

So here we are, like inexperienced lovers in Acting 101.

"How'd it go at the university today?"

Her cell phone keeps vibrating on the table. I could swear that, when she looks at me, her blinking is exaggerated, like in a cartoon movie.

"Smoothly. This year is going well."

That's a lie: this morning, with the help of some third-year students, we scattered more than twenty pounds of animal testicles in the hallway of her department. My phone pings. I pick it up with a smile, cursing my mother's inquisitive persistence, and I read a message from Hugo: *We've destroyed the van of a group of Princesses. No injuries.*

"My mother sends her love. She says when are you going to have lunch and a good chat with her, she misses you," I improvise.

She looks at her phone and frowns. Then she smiles again.

"Tell her I miss her too. And that I promise we'll keep scoring high on the Bechdel test."

"The what?"

"The Bechdel test. You don't know it?"

"No. Doesn't ring a bell."

She answers me and types into her phone at the same time.

"It's a test that evaluates whether a movie or a book passes the requirements of gender inclusivity. You'll love it, *with your strong interest in these things*."

"I'm sure I will."

Chase ensued. Aguirre almost got caught. Now they're burning dumpsters.

"It uses three questions. The first is: Do at least two female characters appear? The second: Do those characters ever speak to each other? The third: If they do speak, is it about something besides a man?"

"Wow. That's fascinating."

"It is. When your mother and I first began to get together, we would always talk about you or your father."

Her cell phone is still vibrating. She looks at it distractedly between sips of wine. I do the same.

"But you guys aren't fictional characters."

"That's true. But it's interesting to apply the test to real life."

I talked to Bruno. They smashed all the windows of Zara Man.

"In real life we talk about everything," I say.

"Of course. But lately your mother's changed. Even I've noticed, and I don't see her very often. For weeks now, she's stopped talking about you guys and we've started talking about...other things."

"What things?"

She laughs with the fakest laugh I've ever heard in my life.

"I don't know, silly billy. Different things. Life, the future...you know. I can't tell you about them, I'd be betraying her confidence."

She raises an eyebrow.

"I'd like to be a fly on the wall," I say.

"You can't. That's the whole point."

I think of vaginas laughing at me.

"Sure, of course. Please, I won't butt in. Besides, it makes me very happy that you are so close with my mother."

You can't imagine how happy.

"She's an incredible woman. It's been a real discovery. Sorry, I have to answer this message."

"Yeah. I see you've very popular tonight."

"It's the professors' group. They're so annoying..."

Downtown is under police command. We're scattering. Ramos is out of control.

I feel nauseated. The red pilot light comes on again: there is something profoundly disgraceful and wrong about what I'm doing. It's starting to become a recurring sensation, which is why I've lost my appetite recently. I wait for Najwa to finish typing, and I serve myself another glass of wine.

"Everything OK?"

"Yeah, yeah," she says. "It's a silly thing. There's a meeting tomorrow and we're preparing our arguments to defeat our opponents."

I don't like what I've just heard, not in the slightest.

"Is it urgent?"

"No, not at all. A typical department meeting. But there's always someone pushing in the opposite direction."

We had to split up. There are too many of them. I counted more than a hundred. They don't care if the police arrest them.

"Well, sounds like tomorrow will be an interesting day."

She looks into my eyes.

We have a fucking problem.

"Undoubtedly," she smiles.

23

GARBO'S HANDS smell like eggs. The irony is not lost on him.

The group rushes into the car, but Ramos doesn't take off.

"Where the fuck is Donovan?" he shouts.

It's true. Donovan isn't there, and they don't see him anywhere nearby. They've lost him somewhere between the demonstration and their parking spot.

"Start the car, for God's sake!" begs Aguirre.

Behind them, other drivers have stopped. There is honking, and voices. The riot police, outnumbered, run from one side to the other. If it weren't for their batons and shields, they would be pitiful.

"Look!" says Hugo.

Some twenty-odd Princesses have appeared out of nowhere, literally. They are wearing their usual masks, which are getting scarier and scarier—scorched at cheek height, melted and coagulated like a black candle—and they are carrying tools for battle: baseball bats, chains, Molotov cocktails. The first ambulance sirens are heard, stores pull down their shutters, people take refuge in doorways. A column of smoke peeks out at the end of the avenue. It smells like tires.

Garbo, anxious to get home, looks up. Then he sees them.

Dozens of flags with M and W on them.

"He knows the escape protocol. He'll find us. Get the fuck out of here already," he says.

Ramos tries to drive away, but the street is blocked off just meters ahead. He veers to the left, entering the opposite lane. Another car comes head-on and stops just before crashing into them. The vehicle remains at a diagonal standstill, unable to move.

"We're trapped," he says.

"We have to leave the car," suggests Garbo.

"Hell no," responds Ramos. "I'm still paying for it, and these bitches are capable of anything."

"And what the fuck do you want to do? Stay here?"

The Princesses are approaching. One of them swings a chain in circles over her head, like a cowboy about to lasso a wayward steer.

"OK. Fuck it. Let's go."

They put their bandannas back on and get out of the car. They run toward a cross street some fifty meters away, camouflaging themselves among the frenzied crowd around them.

"It's Donovan!" Bruno points halfway to the street they're headed toward.

It isn't Donovan: it is a three-way illegal fight in which Donovan is taking part, to be more precise. In the left corner, weighing in at over two hundred pounds, with his back glued to the wall and protected by a bakery sign advertising organic breakfasts, the Krav Maga instructor, the sixth member of the team. In the right corner, weighing in at approximately six hundred pounds spread among six or seven bodies, a band of Princesses in shorts and combat boots, their hair pulled back into buns, wearing terrorific masks and holding unidentifiable objects in their hands. In the center, at 350 pounds of flesh, reinforced plastic, and Kevlar, two riot police armed with batons, striking blows in every direction, unsure of who exactly is the enemy. The Princesses pounce on their backs, tearing off their helmets and trying to snatch their weapons. Donovan protects himself like a boxer, rotating his hips, throwing quick punches with his left fist, covering his face with his forearms, but there are too many of them, and when he manages to somehow make contact with one of their faces, two more grab him by the legs to immobilize him. Slowly, they isolate him between a car and the wall, leaving him defenseless. They have no scruples: they use their fists and their boots, but also their knees, nails, and elbows. One of them has lifted her mask so she can use her teeth. They fight like savages.

"Run! Every man for himself!" screams Garbo. "We can't take them. Hide wherever you can, and we'll meet in half an hour at the car, when everything's blown over."

"And Donovan?" asks Aguirre.

"He's in better shape than all of us put together. He'll survive."

Hugo and Ramos run in opposite directions. Aguirre leans on the car to catch his breath.

"I'm gonna help him," says Bruno.

Garbo stops looking at the chaos surrounding Donovan and walks quickly southward, with the hope of finding a place to hide out until things settle down. The sound of screaming is unbearable. He stumbles on an abandoned shopping cart, and as he walks over it he steps on a carton of milk that explodes with a loud plop. No one reproaches him: people are either recording videos from a certain distance or fleeing, and that's it. It looks like a movie with dozens of extras.

He sees an open door and he goes in. His heart is beating so hard that he can feel it in his eyes—it's like a muscular throbbing that overdosed on oxygen. He exhales. He closes the door without asking permission, turns around and sees what is happening on the other side of the window glass.

More riot police. Princesses running, fleeing them or destroying trash and recycling bins. Men crouching, trying to become invisible. Broken windows. Trash cans uprooted and lying on their side. Cars with their blinkers on, chassis dented like Play-Doh. Women jumping on them, with their fists in the air. Small fires. Tackling. Arrests.

He can't see if Bruno managed to get to Donovan.

"You're scared, huh?" says a voice.

Garbo turns and realizes where he is. It's a hair salon. He makes a quick calculation: two girls in uniform; three women over sixty; a guy with a broom. Friendly territory.

"Shit, it's really getting hairy out there," he responds.

The woman who's asking him is one of the older ones. She has bits of tinfoil on her head.

"You deserve it. All of you."

"Don't say that," interjects another woman. "This boy doesn't have any fault in all this, and look what they're doing to the streets. I'm against it."

"Well, I'm not. I'm all for it. It's about time we women did something."

"Spoken like a true widow."

Garbo doesn't know if he should speak or keep quiet.

Little by little, the noise outside dies down. It seems the Princesses have moved on to another area and dragged the riot police along with them. Through the glass they can see several injured people, but nothing too serious: bruises, superficial gashes, scrapes. Cars begin to move. Before leaving the salon, Garbo asks a general question, like a test.

"Why do we deserve it?"

The first woman smiles, her head reflecting the orange lights from a fire truck.

"Check your privilege, boy."

The air smells of gasoline. Aguirre is leaning on the passenger-side door of Ramos's car, as Ramos approaches from the end of the street. Garbo waves discreetly to them.

"And the others?" asks Aguirre.

"I don't know," says Garbo. "We could wait a little longer."

Ramos approaches, cursing.

"Let's kill those bitches. Let's make their lives impossible. They think they own the streets, that they can do whatever the fuck they want? We're gonna stick them in concentration camps, I swear.

To fuck, suck dick, to do what we tell them to do. Did you see what they did? Hysterical bitches! I've never been more afraid in my fucking life, shit. The minister of the interior better take action. Except for the little girls and the old ladies, the rest can suck my knob. The old ladies, into nursing homes. And careful with the little girls, they wise up fast. Keep them on leashes, like dogs. What fucking world are we living in?"

That's exactly what Garbo was wondering.

Then Bruno shows up, a few meters away, holding Donovan by one armpit, helping him to walk. Aguirre gestures them over. Donovan is in pretty bad shape. His eyes are swollen shut like two big blue balls, there's dried blood on his mouth, and he's got a serious limp. Bruno's shirt is in tatters. When they reach the car, Garbo sees that his face is disfigured by multiple wounds. His cheeks are probably harboring an infection, and will need a few stitches.

"Should we go to the hospital?"

"That's not necessary," stutters Donovan. "To Hugo's house. He must be waiting for us there."

The group gets into the car. Hugo's house is far away, but recovering there seems like the best idea. Ramos, at the wheel, keeps cursing, constantly, as can be inferred by the intensity of Aguirre's prayers: "Forgive him, Father, for he has sinned. And he just keeps on sinning." In the distance, the battle continues: they hear the police voicing a series of requests through megaphones, and the crowd responds with shouting. The city center is chaos. It's hard to drive. Some cars are still stopped in the middle of the street and others are speeding, ignoring the officers and the lights, as if all traffic rules were suspended.

Suddenly, after they get onto a main artery with no jams and Ramos steps on the gas, they come across a group of Princesses who are trying to block the road. Twelve, fifteen. Maybe more. The cars in front of them stop short, with no warning. Ramos turns the steering wheel and slips out along the left lane, slams on the accelerator, runs a stop sign, skids, curses his life, and turns the wheel again to keep from losing traction.

A thud is heard on the passenger-side door.

Ramos steps down hard on the pedal.

"What happened?" screams Bruno.

No one says anything. Garbo looks behind him, squinting his eyes to focus on the pile of female bodies that, as they speed off, grow smaller, and smaller, and smaller.

One of them, on the ground, isn't moving.

24

WE ARE CELEBRATING the fortieth birthday of one
of my best friends. He says: "The worst part is that
I'm as close to twenty as I am to sixty." He's got a
point.

Najwa was planning on coming with me, but
she says her back hurts.

I wonder why.

Phallic State took a week off. After that riot,
we'd earned it. Hugo greeted us at his house with
cigarettes, alcohol, and sandwiches. He told us that
he'd managed to escape by feigning severe mental
retardation, which led to numerous jokes and relaxed the atmosphere. Hugo is good at impressions.
As we ate and drank, we put on the TV: all the
channels were reporting on the riots, mentioning
certain hoaxes that had gone viral and highlighting

the imminent conflict society was likely to be in
for. No: no one sodomized any men. No: no one
was tied to a post. No: the banks weren't affected,
there was no looting or kidnapping.

The group toasted their survival with cham-
pagne and ham, but I had no appetite, eaten up
by anxiety. The only thing I wanted to know was
whether the Princess we'd hit with the car was OK,
or if we had crossed a line that was too much for me
to bear. I waited for each news item with my heart
in a vise, imagining my reaction to the words *dead*,
victim, or *deceased* amid the apathetic laughter of my
companions, until finally, after what seemed like
an eternity, a reporter announced that a twenty-
year-old woman had suffered numerous injuries of
varying gravity from a collision with a car. She was
conscious and mad as hell. She would live. The incident was being investigated. After that I was able
to breathe, and I thought for the first time about
leaving the group. After all, hadn't I fulfilled all
my objectives? I wanted to provoke women: done.
I wanted to piss them off so much that they would
move from pacifist resistance to violent action:
done. I wanted the feminist struggle to become
something solemn: a radical conquest backed by
force, defended by militants who refused to accept
the status quo and who brought about a shift in historic roles: done. Or, at least, that was happening.

The Princesses were multiplying. They were receiving support from everyone. My work was complete. What more could I do? Keep meeting up with
this band of hopeless misogynists? Keep lying to
my loved ones? I decided that I would quit a few
days later, once the euphoria had waned, the buzz
of the high had worn off, so I wouldn't have to give
a lot of explanations.

"Are you OK?" asked the birthday boy.

My breathing is labored, my lungs filled with
questions.

"Yes. Just a little tired. Is there any more wine?"

I feel out of place. I am leading a double life that
my friends—the people I grew up with, whom I trust
more than anyone, and of course my girlfriend—
know nothing about. This is symptomatic: I've
hidden what I'm doing from Najwa because I'm
embarrassed about what I'm doing. It's like living
a lie. I'm incapable of raising a single topic or taking part in any conversation. I move like an invisible insect among these men, who are talking about
their insomnia; their kids, who are running from
the playground toward the fried snacks; and their
wives, who are sitting in a circle nursing babies. I'm
the other, the dregs, the dissonant verse.

"You don't look too good."

He says it lovingly, with the honesty allowed
by our more than twenty years of all-nighters and

awkward drunken bouts. He has no idea how spot-on his analysis is.

"I'm going to get some more wine," I say.

Fear is contagious: it leaps from one person to the other, airborne like a virus.

I decide to go over to the group of women to find out if they are talking about the only subject I'm interested in. Will they support what's going on? Will they condemn the violence? Will child-rearing have made them deaf to the noise of the world? I haven't seen them since that afternoon when I turned a peaceful social gathering into a fabulous quarrel, so I'm not ruling out the possibility they want to avoid me.

Their conversation is almost a collective whisper, because they are all taking part, but in very soft voices, as if they don't want to bother the babies cradled in their arms or be heard by the others. I situate myself at a reasonable distance, not too close and not too far, so they will be aware of my presence but not feel they have to include me.

"A guy tried to rape me in a bar bathroom. When I was fifteen."

"My uncle would feel me up at family dinners, with my parents right there, and they didn't even notice. Or that's what I like to believe."

"I don't know a single woman who hasn't been through something."

I'm unable to distinguish who is saying what. It's a monotone murmur, without compassion, a mere registry of accidents and humiliation, of abuses and crimes. It's like a chorus of the dispossessed, or a photographer's office piled high with dozens of discarded, quotidian pictures no one wants to look at, because they no longer matter, or because they're old, or because there are new photographs, ones with children in them, and toys. The colors are all the same.

"More than once they've made me regret the clothes I was wearing. They've panted in my ear as they rubbed up against me, grabbed one of my breasts in a crowd, tried to kiss me without my consent. They've insulted me for rejecting their propositions. They've insisted, coerced, and blackmailed me into things I found uncomfortable or didn't like. At work, they've forced me to dress a certain way, to be pleasant to those who were crossing the line. When I walk down the street alone, I'm always alert. I avoid certain routes because they make me feel vulnerable. And all this has been going on since I was eleven, since I've had tits, if you can call those little bumps tits, although they were to them, of course, there was no need for them to say it, it showed in the way they looked at me, obscenely, turning my body into an object. We learn it from girlhood: they have the right, any group of men can legitimately say whatever they want to a woman passing by, no matter her age, no matter how she feels. They are protected by a historical jurisdiction. And when you accept that you can say anything, it isn't long before you assume that you can do anything too. That's the point. It's a perfect pyramid."

There is no anger in their words. They don't raise their voices. I'm insulted by their resignation. My throat opens; I can't control it—before I have time to think, my rigorous sense of ethics is selfishly offended, knowing itself to be valid, knowing it has all the answers. It's not my mouth: it is the mouth of a man exercising his role as a man. I'm the stupid guy who starts talking when no one has asked him to.

"What the hell are you talking about? Is this like therapy? This isn't a club, for fuck's sake. You're normalizing violence against women, making teams. I tell you my shit and you tell me yours, and that way we can vent. Why are you so calm? Why don't you get up for once and fucking do something about it? This is fucking embarrassing. You should be angry. You should go out on the street and cut off the head of every man who makes you feel bad, or worthless, or like you're just holes to stick it in. Every single one! How can you talk so nonchalantly about that stuff? It's unfair. It's unfair and dangerous. You are completely wrong."

In my fantasy, my stirring speech fired up their souls. They agreed with me and applauded my efforts. They hugged me tightly. "Well said," one of them would shout, tears in her eyes. "Finally, somebody knows what to do!"

However, my words brought on a different emotional reaction. An unexpected one. They looked at me in silence, as if we existed in different languages, as if we were composed of irreconcilable substances. And, for the first time since I've known them, they react simultaneously, without prior consultation. They slowly stand up, one by one, leave the circle, move away from their children and their horror stories, ignoring me tactfully, without blinking, standing tall, filling with repulsion.

I'm alone. Time stops.

I see Najwa's face like mystics saw the face of God, amid mist, awaiting the truth that will be revealed.

That's me.

That's me explaining to a victim how to stop being one.

That's me explaining to a woman what a victim is.

I'm drowning. I'm drowning in my own thoughts. For months I've been speaking in other people's names. I need air. I run through the tables, not paying attention to my friends or their kids or the chairs. I push a tray of food, which flies through the room creating a rainbow of cheese and bread rolls. I need air. I leave. I disappear.

The red pilot light goes on: I can't even distinguish colors anymore.

My feet move as quickly as the electrical impulses in my brain. The street becomes a racetrack, I lose my peripheral vision, I focus on a distant point on the horizon. My heart drops into my stomach, and from there to my intestine.

Look at you. You are your own summary of crimes: there are the sexual jokes, the usurping, the complicit silences, all the times you didn't listen to what a woman was telling you, your condescension. There you are, using the breadth of your knowledge to return to the original sin, feeling the power you exert over them when you speak, enjoying it: "I want you to obey me, I want to control you, I want to educate you. I want to use what you know to my benefit." You weren't being an ally, but rather a harasser. Your cognitive liberation is a fraud. You've stopped looking at men, when that was where you should focus the brunt of your argument. You've stopped looking at them because they are never the object. You've stopped looking at them because men are the subject of a sentence you've been repeating for decades, in which you are always the verb.

So take a look at yourself.

I stop running when I feel crystals building up inside my legs. I lie down on the ground, face up, trying to open my ribs to give my lungs space.

I feel dizzy.

And before losing consciousness, because I know I will in one or two minutes, I hear breathing around me, as someone tries to move me, as someone calls the paramedics. I move one hand to let them know that I'm OK, that nothing's wrong with me. I just need some air. A little space. Some time to admit that I've behaved like a monster, and therefore, given that it's too late to correct this monstrous reality, this mountain of contradictions that ended up becoming the exact definition of my guilt, it's only fair that I return to the world what I've taken from it, it's only fair that they point at me and chase me, and that my final act of responsibility— my sentence—is to be the monster.

Make me an example, a symbol, a mold to break.

When I get up I am no longer me, and he is no longer Garbo.

PART

THREE

25

BEFORE THE TRUCE cleared the streets and alleviated
the tension that had taken hold in homes and cities
across the country, there had been a constant wave
of spontaneous attacks, protests, looting, barricades,
anonymous aggression, fires, and kidnappings.

Those months were dubbed the Scorched
Revolution.

Women simply took the initiative. The Princesses won over countless people of varying degrees
of radicalism to their cause, who implemented a
daily routine of violence without any transitions
from the previous phase: some neighborhoods became war zones from one day to the next, because
there was no organized core establishing the parameters for the action, merely a grouping of inde-
pendent cells that took part in it like musicians in

a jam session, improvising, sure, but with an un-derlying melody that all the women heard. They wanted to make noise and cause damage, and show that together they were capable of halting and cor-nering the old way of looking at the world. The battle wasn't experienced equally in rich areas as in poor areas, or in cities as in towns, of course, but the fundamental discourse was the same, and its consequences, through contagion, were identi-cal. The media tried to speculate in its way, with programs and articles condemning the violence and applauding the courage of men who stood up to it, although increasingly more outlets aligned them-selves with the revolutionary message. There was talk of a "civil war," of a "state of siege." In more conservative arenas, of "uterine furor." As always happens when a certain drug is legalized in a pu-nitive country, consumption increases for the first few months until it drops and stabilizes—there was a significant uptick in sexist violence that lasted a hundred days: many men, furious at the situ-ation, took it out on their wives, their daughters, their neighbors, searching, perhaps, to balance out the number of victims. After those hundred days, and the targeting and persecution, the men realized that the response from the opposition was growing stronger and bloodier, and their acts of aggression decreased for the first time in recorded history. The

Catholic Church took a harsh stand, excommunicating women in the public sphere by the dozens, until a bishop showed up nude, waxed, and handcuffed to the portico of a cathedral, with his body covered in threats written in red ink, placed in an unforgettable scene: hundreds of pages, photos, and files listing the historical crimes of the clergy against women. Witch hunts, the Inquisition, exorcisms, abuse, rapes, silence. And more. From that point on, the Church devoted itself, with its proverbial circumspection, to praying for the souls of the sinners. The lists, however, continued to flow: they revealed names of abusers and rapists, businessmen and important figures who had stalked or harassed their employees, elite athletes tied to human trafficking rings. It happened suddenly, naturally; the women began to tell everything. Using both first and last names, they made inventories of the insults, beatings, and rapes, standing up with some shame—at first—but later swaddled in conviction that made them seem invulnerable, blameless, focused on placing the weight of their story on the aggressors. They revealed miseries from years ago, abuses, improper dismissals, groping. One in every two men was on a page, or in a newspaper, or in a press release. And the more extensive the catalog of aberrations, the more sordid the list of injustices, the more the Princess masks came off.

There was a policy of constant humiliation, without bloodshed or excessive brutality, except in particular cases. Sure, more than one man died from a heart attack; sure, one or two hurtled down the stairs to their death, trying to escape. Mostly accidents, according to the reports. Except for that group of young men who showed up wounded and bruised in the square of their small town, tied up and gagged. Or that professor, with a habit of biting things he shouldn't, who suffered the extraction of several teeth. Or that doctor, with all the broken fingers. Unlike those isolated cases, carried out by vigilantes with a very specific personal history, the bulk of the actions were divided into three big blocks.

First of all, the war on the street, which affected big- and medium-sized cities just as much as tiny towns: destruction of street furniture; blockading businesses with a surplus of men in executive positions; impeding access to infrastructure and taking reprisals against the supporters of Phallic State. Second, the dronification of the conflict: attacks studied and planned with surgical precision against particular targets, generally men with political power who repudiated—in their words or actions—the problems stemming from the women's uprising. For their positions, they usually only received attention-grabbing displays of affection, such as a shower of red paint, some creative embellishment on their cars, a broken window or a daily serenade beneath it. Third, there was the political propaganda and vindication: in addition to the increasing lists and accusations, the self-proclaimed leaders of the insurrection revealed—in the national and international media—a series of basic demands that had to be met before they'd order an end to the violence and begin a process of dialogue that, over time, could build a space of mutual tolerance and respect. No one knows the internal process that lead to the unmasked appearance of those dozen, wildly varied women on television, although it would be reasonable to imagine that it wasn't easy to pull off, due to the apparent multiplicity and the various fronts that composed the movement; but that was in fact one of their first lessons: the hierarchical order, the illusion of balance, of a system regulated by closed structures, was part of the universe they were trying to dissolve. The patriarchy was unable to comprehend that. The demands included a wide spectrum of requests. Some were practical in nature, like the immediate elimination of the wage gap, the tip-to-toe reform of the gender-based violence law (basically swapping protection of the women for control of the men), and including all men in maternity leave, to eradicate gender discrimination in the working world; others were symbolic: amendments to the canonical dictionaries, to remove all that linked the feminine with delicateness, weakness, and gentleness; or the commitment to gender-neutral language—the changes that were more complicated to explain forced a reworking of models that our society had deeply internalized, like how women's health is seen by the medical establishment; scientific and pharmaceutical research linked to female sexuality, reproduction, and motherhood; mandatory quotas in all public and private spheres; and the establishment of a specific, all-female security corps to safeguard the constitutional rights and needs of women.

The state reacted in two stages. At first, it tried to intervene as if the situation were exceptional and transitory, increasing the police presence in large cities and putting down, by force, any illegal activity. Soon they understood two things: that there were not enough officers to cover the whole country, and that neither the district attorney's office nor the prisons could keep up with the number of daily arrests and reports. According to the statistics, for every woman who went into jail, two more took her place on the streets. The groups of men, who at first had fought against the Princesses in a disorganized way, found themselves overwhelmed and began to disappear, even going so far as publicly declaring their regret and joining the ranks of their former rivals. That forced the state to take measures: they decided to mobilize the army. But, in an unusual declaration on live television that spurred the women on, the head of state declared his own rebellion, not accepting the government's requirement and suggesting a three-month interruption of activities, with minimum services, so that an alternative could be found. As a result, 90 percent of the women registered with Social Security joined a historic strike, and the entire country ground to a halt. Many businesses closed. Hospitals and schools, overwhelmed by the lack of workers, began to accept, against the official position of the administration, the women's demands. The international press echoed the disaster. The president went into hiding. The ministers were unable to give any explanation. The atmosphere became unbearable: it seemed a probably tragic massive popular uprising was imminent, and no one knew what the outcome would be. And then, the lower house of Parliament, without the support of its more reactionary members but with a large majority, at a special session that lasted almost thirty hours, opened up a channel of communication with the leaders of the Scorched Revolution, without conditions or threats, to mitigate the economic collapse and inaugurate a new era based on equality, parity, and justice. An unlimited truce was established. The women formalized an exclusively feminist political party, without the a priori ambition to govern, but just to be a microphone and link to the needs of more than half the population, needs that had been ignored for so many centuries. Their plan was relentless, but the exceptional conditions the country was facing necessitated early elections that placed the Princesses as the fourth-largest political force in the nation and made their atypical political appearance key to the formation of the parliamentary government. At this point, all the political scientists and specialists concurred in their diagnosis: there was no way to take power without the backing of the Princesses' party.

The conversations lasted weeks, but finally a government coalition was created. The Princesses had popular support and a considerable number of seats in the Parliament, and after several months, the constitution was amended according to most of their demands. Amnesty was declared for all the women in the movement who were still in prison. Dumpsters, which remained a common target for the sector most skeptical of the Princesses, stopped burning. Schools ruled out adding more security guards at their front doors. Peace came slowly, when they made space for it.

The country entered a new era.

Nevertheless, Phallic State, still active in the city where it was dreamed into existence by its earliest members, like a trace residue that refused to accept society's undeniable sea change, and assuming—through communiqués and small subversive operations—the mantle of the Resistance, did not lay down their weapons.

They still believed they could win the war.

They were just waiting for the perfect moment.

26

VERGO AND HIS COMRADES hide in a small, old apartment downtown, with just one bathroom. They sleep on cots and take turns cooking and showering. Since the Truce began they no longer need to shop in pairs, or worry about the condition of their cars. They behave like a sleeper cell of commandos. The female neighbors believe they are a group of contractors with staggered shifts, hired by a renovations company, which explains their strange schedules. They don't play music, or host parties, or call attention to themselves.

They always speak in a whisper.

"I'm still afraid when I go to certain places," says Ramos as he dresses a salad. "Last night, on my way home, I took a shortcut down a narrow street, the one on the left. I wanted to get here as fast as I could. And holy fuck."

"Did they recognize you?" asks Bruno.

"No. But I felt I was being watched. There was a group of women in front of a bar, smoking. My age. I lowered my head, but I could totally feel how they were watching me. All of them. If they'd recognized me, I doubt I could have escaped."

"Vengeful bitches, vindicative bitches..." says Donovan.

Aguirre stops cutting bread and waves his hands through the air, drawing the others' attention without raising his voice.

"Don't use those words! Are you crazy? You want them to hear us, you idiot? You want them to realize who we are and what we're doing?"

"And what do you want me to do?" complains Donovan. "Sorry! I'm really sorry. But this isn't easy for me, alright? You've taken away half of my...of my..."

"Vocabulary," says Ramos. "Relax, kiddo. I know how you feel. And you, altar boy, take it easy. We whisper so damn much I can barely hear myself, so take it down a notch."

"All I'm saying is that we need to protect the apartment. Behave, I'm begging you. I'm the one who goes to the supermarket most days. You think

I don't hear them talking, don't see them looking at me suspiciously? They do, believe me they do: I look a lot like that photograph of me online. But if they say anything, I smile and go about my business. And nothing happens. We're in a truce."

"My teeth hurt from smiling so much," says Donovan.

Bruno tries to encourage him with a pat on the shoulder. He misses spending time in gay bars, and Donovan's the only thing keeping him sane. They aren't as fit as they were, because they haven't been going to the gym, but they are still the group's brawn and share their old complicity. Aguirre and Ramos, on the other hand, are terribly skinny, with enormous bags under their eyes; they haven't shaved in so long that they can scarcely recognize themselves in the mirror. At least it makes it easier for them to get around in public.

There's a knock at the door: two, one, three.

That's the code.

When Bruno opens up, Hugo falls into his arms.

"Thank you, thank you..." he whispers, coughing, his face ashen.

"What happened?"

"They almost...they almost got me. The FeCuntGuard."

Aguirre waves his hands again.

"Don't call them that! It's the Female Constitutional Guard. The FeConGuard. Are you all deaf?"

Working together, they move around the chairs so that Hugo has more space. He lies down on the sofa, with his legs up, on the armrest. They are waiting for him to catch his breath. Aguirre fans him with a newspaper from the previous week. On its front page a headline reads EUROPE TAKES NOTE.

"It was a mistake... Don't tell Vergo, please."

"What'd you do this time?" asks Ramos.

"I was meeting with one of our contacts... The actor, you know who I mean. We agreed on the next package, day, time, place. Everything was set. But, of course, we also had a couple of drinks, to let off some steam. Like we used to, in the old days. Maybe more than a couple. I was wearing the fake moustache, you know. I felt safe. And before I left I passed a couple of young chicks..."

"No..."

"What'd you do?" asks Aguirre.

Hugo doesn't respond.

"What the hell did you do, you sick fuck?" insists Bruno.

"I... Fuck, I don't know how it happened... It was the alcohol, I swear... And it wasn't that big a deal. They walked past me and..."

"Just fucking say it!"

"I don't remember it clearly! OK? I said something to them. Your mouth would look good around my cock, or some shit like that. It just slipped out. It was a fucking compliment! Anyway, almost immediately I had a ton of chicks on top of me, taking photos, hounding me, kicking me out of the bar on my ass. And somebody must have called the FeConGuard, one of those damn whores, because as I was leaving I heard the siren, that fucking siren that sends my balls crawling up inside me, and a car showed up, and out came two huge FeCons the size of Donovan, and I ran off, I didn't even know where I was, shit, and it was just a joke, I don't know...Don't tell Vergo, please."

"Did they catch you? Did they recognize you?" asks Aguirre.

"No! There's no way!"

"You and your big fucking mouth..." complains Bruno.

"I swear, they didn't!"

The office door opens, silencing Hugo's whining. It's the only room that no one enters without permission.

Vergo has a scar that starts on his upper lip, goes across his right cheek and to his eye. He shaves his head every day, giving him the appearance of a hostile inmate used to not seeing the sun, a lone wolf. On his chest is a tattoo of an enormous penis:

the testicles—depicted as hand grenades—float on either side of his navel, and the shaft—pointy and shaped like an arrow, the head covered in blood—reaches his throat, just below his Adam's apple. On his back are two women on their knees, their faces at the ground and their asses in the air, kissing the feet of an unidentifiable man with open arms, who could very well be Vergo himself. He has a slight limp and black fingernails.

Every member of the group owes him their life, and he's paid the price. Which is one of the reasons why he refuses to answer to his former name, Garbo. Garbo died long ago.

"Everything set up with the actor?" he asks.

No one says anything. Hugo nods in silence.

"When will we have the material?"

"Thursday... At midnight. In the building."

Vergo nods and gestures for them to sit around the table. He has the air of both a shaman and a doctor: he could invoke the rain or define a cancer cluster with the same grim, phlegmatic, merciless expression. The group obeys him out of inertia.

"I know it's been difficult," he begins. "Everything that happened to us before the Truce, the fights, the injuries, the scars... We're still recovering, and there are some things we'll never get over. We've left behind our lives, our families, our jobs. We live in a shitty apartment. We barely have any money coming in. I know it hurts not to see your children, Aguirre, and Donovan, I know you miss your parents. I also know that all of you are nervous about the future: I've divided up the tasks individually, without giving you much information, demanding your complicity and your silence, and right now none of you know what the others are working on, or whether your efforts will pay off. Forgive me. I didn't do it this way because I don't trust you, but just to keep us all safe. I trust each and every one of you. But I wanted to protect the information so that, if anybody got found out, or—in the worst-case scenario—captured by the enemy and interrogated, our plan could still continue. And I say "our" plan because it's not my plan, I'm just its architect. It's ours because we share a common idea, a vision of the world. It's ours because we are going to put our lives in service to a cause that's bigger than us."

Ramos is about to start crying. The others stifle their emotion as best they can.

"So, all this, this apartment, this living like pariahs, this constant fear of being ourselves, of going out on the street, is there any point to it? Is there any future?"

Vergo smiles. He's missing a tooth. Two.

"Of course. I promise we'll get back what belongs to us. Because it's ours. Because it will always be ours. Because if we can't have it, no one can."

27

NAJWA ENTERS the office confidently. She isn't intimidated by the portraits hanging on the walls, or the ornate wooden desk, or the immaculate Persian carpet that muffles the sound of her steps. Her colleagues are waiting in the next room, with the ministers and the delegates, because this meeting must be private. Just her and the president, no one else. All the groundwork is done, and now all that's left is to look into each other's eyes, confirm the commitments with a handshake, and make the appropriate documents public. Set the scene, because theater is politics too.

"Coffee?"

"I prefer Red Bull. If you have it. It's hard for me to get moving in the morning."

"It's hard for all of us."

The president is a professional politician, a chess player toiling away at the calculation of possibilities and anticipating moves, and although he has to admit that initially he made the mistake of underestimating the scope of the conflict, and that he acted precipitously, perhaps poorly advised by his counselors, right now the meeting with Najwa seems like an extraordinary opportunity to remain in power, win the admiration of a good number of voters, and increase his popularity. Even beyond borders: he will lead the first Western government that advocates a policy of indisputable, revolutionary equality; it'll be studied in the history books of the future. However, in his opinion, there are still a few loose ends that need to be dealt with to make the blueprint as perfect as possible. That's why he's called this meeting.

"According to the press, we are still in a truce."

"I know."

Beyond the office, and the other offices, and past all the people waiting expectantly for the meeting to end, some three or four kilometers away from Najwa and the president, the first vans filled with men are arriving at an old building that once—in a bygone time, when paper was still important— housed one of the largest presses in the country.

"We've introduced practically all the demands presented to us, and some of the ones proposed by the parliamentary groups themselves, into the new constitution. The Royal Academy of Language has modified the ideologically outdated terms. Just yesterday I saw a first-division match with a female referee, which is starting to be normal for fans, if you'll permit me a frivolous example. It's true that some of the more complex topics, the economic ones, are slower in coming, but by the end of the year all the companies will have adopted the new model. You already know all this, of course. What I mean is that the government has a firm commitment to continued progress, working together to establish a lasting framework of coexistence. Are you, and the other women, satisfied?"

Are they satisfied? Najwa mentally reviews the microvictories they've won recently: reports of abuse, sexual violence, and stalking have decreased by six points and counting, thanks to the radical policies that make visible the consequences of the culture of contempt and other symbolic injustices. Now no one dares to justify or publicly minimize any aggression toward women, and doing so is a crime. People have begun to understand that gender-based violence is not a consequence of inequality, but a structural pillar of a world we'd created. And a certain normality has settled in the streets, with women walking home alone and unafraid without changing their route to avoid particular areas. There is a strong feeling of belonging and solidarity, supported by the many men who now understand the extent to which they'd excluded women, discriminated against them, and deprived them of their rights, giving them the status of an unequal subject. Harassment has basically disappeared from bars, nightclubs, public spaces; in fact, there have been some creative approaches: there are more and more places that clearly indicate whether flirting is allowed; there's a new trend of colored bracelets to reveal one's sexual preference, relationship status, and openness (or lack thereof) to establishing contact, and "no means no" has been taken to heart to a large extent. Respect has become a mantra, because many men have accepted the conflict they felt around women's autonomy and have done some soul-searching; the idea of "consent" has been reformulated, including the consideration of essential parameters such as need and social disadvantage. The salary gap has been reduced, sometimes entirely, in the administration and in small- and medium-sized businesses; mandatory quotas have modified discourse in the media, and at conferences and festivals; housework has been added to taxable economic activities and is renumerated with a minimum wage. Gender blindness has led to an—albeit still meager—awakening of men committed to the revolution. Women have more money, spend more, and dress however they want: the economy is more buoyant, and fashion is going through a transformation unseen since the advent of jeans. Yes: they are moderately satisfied.

"There's still a lot to be done," she responds.

The president nods calmly and circumspectly.

"Of course. And I would like for us to do it together."

Cars arrive, along with the vans. They park where they can, because the lot beside the building is full. When they turn off the motor, they wait. The instructions are clear: no more than two men can congregate around the printing press building at the same time. The occupants of the vehicles get out one by one, looking at the ground, distracted, as if thinking about something insignificant. If they see another man, they dawdle to give him time: tying a shoe, playing with their phone, lighting a cigarette. Above all, serenity.

"In any case," continues the president, "there are two or three matters I'd like to clear up with you, if you don't mind."

"Of course not. That's why we're here. What is it?"

The president likes that she is direct. She doesn't like that he is so dripping with honey, but ever since she took off her mask and her identity became public, ever since she accepted the challenge of being the spokesperson for the movement she had helped create, she was used to the pomp and circumstance, to extended hands, to theatrical smiles. If only it would all end soon and she could delegate, and return to her thesis, which she can barely recall at this point, and stop giving interviews and listening to all the stories of women who come up to her on the street, and at cafés, and online. But she doubts that will happen.

"First of all, I would like the Truce to become a definitive end to hostilities. Agreed to in writing."

"We haven't employed violence in a long while. Unless Phallic State does something, in which case the women simply respond. Until they stop."

"That's true, of course. But society needs to know that the Truce is over, and not because, how can I put this... we haven't reached an agreement, but because there is no longer any need for conflict. We want a peaceful, solid country. Phallic State has become anecdotal, in general terms. And I believe it is fundamental to declare that we are united. That we are changing. That we are going to change even more."

"OK. Everyone is waiting for something, some action, I'm not sure what. Since our teams began to meet, that's all people talk about. What do you have in mind? A press conference?"

"Maybe something a bit more festive. A celebration. The polls show that people want a historic day, and that the media are counting on that. There are parades scheduled for next weekend already, and we should take advantage of the opportunity, for them to celebrate with us. You know what I mean. Not exactly with us. We would be on a stage, someplace special."

"That sounds fine to me."

"There's a 'but.'"

"I suppose there must be. Otherwise, you wouldn't be choosing your words so carefully."

The president smiles for half a second.

"The masks," he says.

"What about the masks?"

"We'd like you to set them aside. There are still women using them. My niece had a birthday party the other day, and all her friends were wearing them. It has us concerned."

"I don't understand. Why?"

"Because they represent a time, a…an activism, let's say, linked to violence. If we are entering a new phase, we should leave behind the formulas that remind us of what we did wrong."

Najwa is silent, thinking. She insinuates with a gesture that she wants to smoke, even though she knows it's not allowed. The president gets up and opens a window.

"If you give me one, I won't say a word," he whispers.

Najwa takes a first drag. "Listen. As is often said, I understand your position, but I don't share it. The answer is no. A firm no."

The president smokes too. She continues.

"Societies are constructed around symbols that mark the collective imagination, and those symbols are, simultaneously, both memory and commitment. Memory of the achievements made and commitment to maintaining the ideals that brought them about. If you, or your government, are made uncomfortable by the masks, you'll have to live with that. Catholics wear chains with a guy nailed to a cross and his head run through with thorns, for fuck's sake. Excuse my bluntness. These masks aren't swastikas, they don't represent a totalitarian principle, but rather its opposite: a radically democratic aspiration. We never wanted to invert the power structure, we want to end power relationships. And don't worry, if we do it correctly, gradually we'll see fewer and fewer girls in masks on the street. Time passes and people forget. But they won't disappear, I can promise you that: they'll be in the homes of all the women who fought to earn a space they never let us occupy. They'll be on doors, in museums, and in universities. They'll be embroidered on your niece's wedding dress. They'll be sold as brooches for elegant ladies. That is what it means to leave a record of what we achieved, Mr. President, what it means to never forget."

The president stubs out his cigarette.

"So I shouldn't even ask about the flags hanging in windows, right?" He smiles.

Najwa bursts into laughter, so hearty it can be heard in the room next door, and in the next one over, and in the next one after that, and all the people inside those rooms sigh with relief, and hug each other, and shout, and someone opens a drawer and uncorks a bottle that's passed from hand to hand and from mouth to mouth, because there aren't enough cups.

And several kilometers from there, an identical—although uneven—scene is taking place.

There are also many people hugging and shouting, and sharing more than one bottle, and cigarettes, and they are also celebrating seeing each other after a long time apart. And the building they are in, the former printing press, turns into an impromptu party, with songs and laughter. And in the middle, like a totem that no one gets near, is a burning Princess flag. And when all that's left of it is a little mound of dust, the men once again occupy the center of the space, the center of the room, and their boots get covered in ash, but nobody cares, because it's just ash, and ash can easily be wiped off with a rag.

28

ONCE ALL THE PIECES are fit together, the plan makes sense. It's complex, risky, and—for some— humiliating, but it makes sense.

Men have come from many different neighborhoods, from nearby cities, from other provinces. Vergo calculates more than a hundred, and he's pleased, although he would have liked to have more, not only to increase the scope of the attack and the number of victims, but also just to give them all some proof that there is still hope. That they are not an island. That they can get back the things that've been taken from them.

There aren't the big swinging dicks there used to be, he thinks when he counts them for the second time.

It's six in the morning.

On October 26th. The day chosen to end the Truce.

Today the National Equality Declaration will be announced.

At one p.m., all the members of the government and the opposition, headed by the president, will accompany the leaders of the Princess movement on a stage set in the green heart of the city, a vast park, more than two hundred acres, designed and built in the 17th century, where both sides would make the peace accord official, using a text already leaked to the media, ushering in a new era of respect, parity, and justice.

"Justice, my big hairy ball sack," says Hugo.

The act will be televised live, and as is to be expected, the site will be guarded by all the state security forces, in particular the Female Constitutional Guard, whose contributions on such a representative day will be especially important. Citizens are called to participate in a day that is projected to be widely attended and joyful. The streets have therefore been under surveillance since the night before, and no vehicles have been allowed into the park's surrounding areas. A thousand porta-potties have been set up, and there is exclusive licensing for small vendors of food and drink in every neighborhood. From this day on, the 26th of October will be a national holiday.

Vergo has divided the men into two groups.

On one hand, the skinniest ones. Hairless, at least in visible parts, except on their heads. Relatively small, but muscly. They have to be able to run when necessary. They are called Princes.

On the other hand are all the rest. Approximately two for every Prince. These guys are called Dragons.

Aguirre was the only Prince who refused to accept his role.

"I got moral problems with this," he said.

"Because of the outfit?" asked Ramos.

"No...the thing itself. I don't think it's right."

Vergo interrupted them.

"Would you be more comfortable being a Dragon?"

"No."

"So what the fuck do you want to do? Are you going to leave us hanging now? You miss your wife, or what?"

He seemed to be speaking without moving his lips, like a ventriloquist. Aguirre immediately crumbled.

"Sorry. I'll be a Prince. Sorry."

End of discussion.

Ramos looked good with the tits on. Aguirre didn't. The group of Princes is made up of twenty-eight men. Bruno and Donovan, who are used to body beautification from their years of going to the gym, painstakingly supervise all the elements of the uniform.

Footwear: women's sneakers. Meaning with sparkles and pastel-colored stripes. Pink or purple laces.

Costume: a skirt, culottes, or a dress. With the skirts, thick stockings and a sweater. With the culottes, wide T-shirts and blouses. With the dresses, a coat.

Accessories: bracelets, painted nails, necklaces, earrings. Wigs, of course.

Structure: sports bra with tits built in. The skinnier Princes were also forced to wear adult diapers padded with socks, so their hips will be reminiscent—given the limits of the imagination—of a woman's.

"Should we put makeup on them?" asks Donovan.

"Yes," replies Vergo.

"Fuck that," says Ramos. "We'll be wearing masks! Isn't shaving enough?"

"We can't be too careful, my friend. If you lose your mask, your best chance is to run and trust they don't notice you're a man. Donovan: distribute lipstick, blush, and eye shadow. Let's forget about mascara, I don't want them to have any trouble seeing."

At eleven, all the Princes were ready.

Seen from a distance, as a group, without masks but already dressed and wearing wigs, with their fake boobs and their diapers, they look like dumpy musicians from an eighties New Romantic band who'd seen better days and were using makeup to hide the dark under-eye circles they'd gotten from lack of sleep or excessive drug use.

Vergo gives them the final instructions.

"Put on women's deodorant, but not perfume. We don't want you to attract too much attention. I'm leaving it in your hands. Don't run, except when it's all over. If you have to use the bathroom, do it now. Exit one by one, in five-minute intervals. Blend in with people, and don't talk to each other, or anyone. Remember: you're mute. Take advantage of groups in costume, with signs, where you can go unnoticed. Try to walk like women. Don't scratch your balls. Don't sit with your legs open. Got it?"

The answer is unanimous: yes.

"On this table you'll find three things. First, a card with the address where you should station yourselves. I want you each to read it, memorize it, and then throw it into this wastepaper basket. We cannot leave any evidence. Memorize it well. If any of you mess up, it could ruin everything we've been working on. You get it?"

Yes, they get it.

"The second is a radio and some earphones. They are all tuned to the same channel. Don't touch the buttons. When you leave here, I want you to put in the earphones, turn on the radio, put your mask on and forget the world. Do you all know the signal to start the show? You remember it?"

Yes, they remember it.

Now he addresses the Dragons.

"Your materials are on the table. A cell phone for each of you. They're charged. The same location cards as the other guys. But don't get too close to each other. Keep your distance. When everything starts, toss the papers. Here they are: take as many as you can. Do it when the shouting starts, but don't lift your arms. We don't want you to be filmed. Drop them over several meters. And then pull out the phones and start recording. Filming the victims. Especially the victims. If one of the Princes enters the frame, hold it for a second or two and then shift. We want images of violence, aggressions. People on the ground. Wounded. When you have them, put away your phones, approach your Prince and get him out of the crowd. It will be chaos: use that to your advantage. Don't let them hurt him. Run to his side quickly. Is that clear?"

Yes, it's clear.

He returns to the Princes one last time.

"The third object on the table is a weapon. There are different kinds: brass knuckles, short-blade knives, expandable batons. Keep them in your pockets until the moment comes. I know it'll be difficult, but remember: we don't want to kill anybody. The idea is to inflict damage, send people to the hospital, but not the cemetery. If you have a blunt instrument, aim at the knees, or the jaw. If you have a sharp one, aim at the arms, the back, soft areas. Don't really stab anyone unless your life is in danger. That's what we've been training for this whole week. We want blood, but not *pools of blood*. OK?"

Yes, OK.

"Come back here when you can. Don't worry about being seen: it'll be so chaotic that no one will notice you. Hugo and I will give you clean clothes and we'll upload the videos online, once we've had a chance to look at them. If for whatever reason you don't think you'll be able to complete the task, come back immediately. This is a safe house. Use it."

Vergo lights a cigarette.

"Any questions?"

No one responds. It's twelve on the dot.

"Go on, then. Let's destroy this shitty fucking utopia."

29

HE HAS TROUBLE breathing through the mask. The women's clothing is a pain. The fake boobs move up and down and are heavier than he'd imagined, but they look real, even without nipples. He groped them a couple of times without meaning to, pure instinct. Luckily, nobody noticed.

And nobody could have, really: the streets are a whirl of colors and people, entire families, babies in strollers, whistles, balloons, drum circles, uniformed groups, squads with thematic costumes, wigs, masks, puppets, couples dancing, musicians, signs. It smells of sweat and cotton candy and fast food, like in an amusement park, and of wine and beer, like at street fairs. He's gotten stepped on several times. And pushed. And asked to dance and offered drinks.

It reminds him of the August festivals in the town he grew up in.

It's hard to walk through the euphoric crowd, and so he moves like a snake, zigzagging, sometimes leaning on a stranger's body and pushing off, carefully leaping over toys and plastic cups, avoiding bottled up areas. He can feel his makeup growing damp under the mask. A baby shrieks in the arms of a young woman. He wishes he could scratch himself.

Aguirre turns up the radio volume.

The preselected station is retransmitting the event taking place inside the park. Right then a female minister is extolling the economic advantages of achieving equality. After every two or three sentences she's forced to stop speaking by the crowd's applause. There seems to be a throng of people around the stage she's on. It can't be too long before the signal comes.

After much effort, Aguirre arrives at the location he's been assigned, drenched in sweat, blinking very quickly to alleviate the irritation in his eyes and to be able to see through the holes in his mask. If he slips up, Vergo will make him pay dearly. So he turns, looks up, looks down, and turns again, as many times as he needs to, until he is sure that yes, he's in the right spot, no doubt about it. It's a wide street, very long and packed with people, that's perpendicular to a narrower pedestrian street. His spot is on a corner, an intersection.

He can't help thinking about the Son of God, his Lord, crucified.

He sticks his hand into one pocket and strokes the weapon he was randomly assigned: a knife. It's not very big, two and a half, maybe three inches. With his thumb he checks that it's nice and sharp. He's been carrying it open since he left the building, so that he can act quickly when the moment comes and not be fumbling with it at the last minute. That could be dangerous, with his nerves. They'd taught him how to hold it correctly and a few basic movements: up/down, right to left, nothing too complicated; everyone knows he's not skilled with tools and they won't be able to turn him into an expert gangbanger in one day. He dries his hand on his dress. What scares him, what keeps him up at night, is screwing up, losing his weapon, failing like always, making a fool of himself in front of his Dragons. He has to be capable of, at least, getting in a stab. Two if he wants to be a hero.

There's Bruno, he notices, several feet away. He is wearing a denim hat and an orange lei, to blend into his surroundings. If he smiled, he'd seem like just another demonstrator, someone waiting for his friends or simply out to enjoy the joyful atmosphere, but he doesn't: he has the same boxer's face as always. The wad of papers makes a bulge in his coat like an erection. Donovan can't be far away.

The president finishes his speech, and Najwa takes the microphone.

The gathered crowd, who can see her on gigantic screens, bursts into cheers and applause. A trumpet sounds. A rain of confetti falls from some window, surrounding the children with flying crystals.

The moment is approaching.

...because it is the work of all women and all men to put an end to power roles...

Aguirre grips his knife.

...this day will be remembered by future generations...

He pulls it out.

...a world in which men and women can live, for the first time, in peace.

Now.

He has to search out a man. Someone his size, distracted, who won't see it coming. He looks to his right: women, teenagers. He looks to his left: got him. About sixty years old, potbellied, wearing a beret. He's holding hands with a woman the same age, probably his wife. He is a reasonable target.

Some fifty meters away the first screams are heard.

His comrades have begun to act.

Aguirre takes two steps toward the man in the beret and stretches his arm back. When he is right behind him, he lets loose against his belly with a fast, slanted jab that enters the flesh of the man's left breast, slashing it, runs along his ribs and exits, practically clean, at the height of his liver. The blood comes shortly after, wetting his plaid shirt from inside, darkening its colors, while the perplexed man watches Aguirre continue walking. His wife, in the moments prior to an anxiety attack, uselessly attempts to cover his wound with her purse.

Then the woman screams. And her screams form a chorus with the distant screams from every direction, and the crowd then becomes a headless, agitated mass of legs and arms and noise, that runs like a single animal, the fear spreading like wildfire, and Aguirre runs with them, feeling his heart grow and beat between his fake boobs, and as he runs he crashes into strange bodies and thinks that nothing matters anymore, that it's fine if they catch him, because the damage is already done, he's attacked one of his own, a man like him—perhaps resigned, perhaps enslaved by the new thinking, yes, but a man after all—so he keeps moving the knife and cutting what he can, whatever's in front of him, joints, forearms, thighs, whatever, ashamed and guilty, and as he runs and slices he senses that Donovan and Bruno are running by his side, even though he can't see them because the mask impedes his vision, that they are pushing him out of the crowd, out of the wailing and tears, out of the maelstrom of obstacles, falls, and fractures, and Aguirre looks at the ground, to know where to step, and throws the knife, and sees it bounce against the concrete and then come to rest, with a muffled sound, beside the thousands of papers that his comrades have scattered through the streets, white, yellow, now trampled by the unpredictable mob.

ONLY WHEN WE CUT OFF THE HEAD
OF THE LAST MAN
WILL WE BE IN PEACE
M   FREEDOM FOR WOMEN   W
FIGHT OR DIE

When he enters the narrow street that crosses the avenue, he stops. He leans against the wall to slow his breathing, his hands resting on his knees, trembling, while fleeing people run past him as fast as they can. He doesn't look at them, he doesn't want to look at anyone, because he knows that God is looking at him.

"Don't stop now," whispers Donovan. "We have to get to the building."

Aguirre can hardly get the words out.

"I need…air…"

"Run, goddamnit!"

Donovan's scream spurs him on. It's true: he has to get out of there. The police and the FeConGuard will arrive soon, and if they look closely at him, they'll realize he's a man disguised as a woman. That would raise suspicions, so he runs off as best he can. He doesn't feel able to make up an explanation. His dress weighs twice what it did before. All sorts of people pass him by: fat, old, disabled. Bruno is a few meters ahead, without the hat but still wearing the lei. He gestures at Aguirre so that he'll follow him.

The building is still pretty far away, so Aguirre stops his progress every few minutes to rub his sharp muscle pains, before starting up again with clumsy movements. His Dragons keep him in their sights. Several blocks from the scene of his attack he changes pace and starts walking, blending into the rhythm and speed of some of those around him. Sirens and skidding tires are heard. Megaphones trying to channel the stampede. He doesn't look back. The party's over.

Still wearing his mask, he crosses the threshold into the building, where there are already many of his comrades, most of them still dressed as women. Hugo and Vergo are giving out little bottles of water and invite them to move inside, to clear the doorway. Others are watching from posts at the windows, through the wooden planks that cover them. A man wearing glasses keeps a list of the number of agents who've returned.

"Still one missing!" he shouts.

Vergo nods and continues handing out provisions to the new arrivals.

Gradually the street empties.

Aguirre drinks down the last sip of his little bottle of water. He wants more.

"Where's Ramos?" he asks.

The street is completely empty. Too empty.

"Where the fuck is Ramos?"

30

HUGO UPLOADED the best videos, using the fake identities they'd been working on for weeks. They showed numerous aggressions by masked women against anonymous men, peaceful protestors who were enjoying the party, fathers, old men with canes, grandpas surrounded by their grandkids. Almost all of the images he selected offer a blurry profile of the woman attacking, in shifting frames, as the camera jerks violently, yet they all clearly, almost definitively, show that the attacker is a Princess. The sound of the screams is deafening. You can see bloodied men on the ground, trampled women, gashes on foreheads, lost shoes, abandoned purses, and an overturned, empty wheelchair. You can see monstrous wounds, eyes swollen like black snails, skinned knees, deep cuts, noses in places where they don't belong. There is a man with his face covered in staples, terrified. There is a man who's lost several incisors. There is a man with his ear dangling, who doesn't know if he should rip it off completely or hold it on, begging someone to call an ambulance.

The repercussion is immediate.

#MurderingPrincesses
#FreeMen
#FeministTerrorists

At the same time, Hugo runs a bot with hundreds of profiles of women who don't exist, radical feminist warriors, Princesses who disagree with the Declaration and support the attacks.

#DeathToAllMen
#PeaceImpossible
#ThisIsWar

In minutes, the videos go viral and reach the media, who broadcast them over and over, warning viewers about their graphic content. Talk show guests, thinking they were going to be commenting as part of an unambitious, saccharine panel, squirm in their chairs as they try to interpret, despite their shock, what is going on, getting into bitter arguments with the other guests, announcing the beginning of a new terrorist model. Some are conciliatory and try to examine the situation with perspective: "These are isolated cases"; others are fatalistic: "I knew this was going to happen"; most don't even try to hide their anger: "We've been tricked," "The government must take measures," "Women deserve to be made an example of." Television studios are filled with men in a way that hadn't been seen in months, with suits and ties, with beards and moustaches. Women disappeared suddenly, vanishing from one video to the next, relegated to a corner of the screen beneath the surtitle "Live."

"Success!" shouts Hugo.

The soldiers are in front of the screens that Vergo and the others brought, enjoying the extraordinary spectacle. The crunching of beer cans, encouraging voices, and the constant murmur of anecdotes of violence are heard: how did you escape, that's what I did, you should have seen his face, when do we do it again. Bruno is kissing one of them in a corner. It's the locker room of a team that just won the championship. It smells like metal and feet.

The government is going to make a statement, obviously, but what everyone is waiting for is Najwa, who hasn't spoken publicly since the act in the park was abruptly canceled by the security forces. Vergo isn't smiling. He is behind his comrades, standing, smoking one cigarette after the other, with a bottle of water in one hand. He timidly accepts congratulations, lowering his head: he is the humble hero, the warrior who doesn't exploit his victory.

Aguirre takes him by the arm and leads him away from the group.

"Ramos is missing," he says.

"I know."

"Aren't you worried? What if they've arrested him?"

"Ramos is smart. They may have arrested him, but I doubt it. The operation was designed to create such chaos that it would be impossible to detect us. If they somehow have, Ramos can always say he likes to dress in women's clothing. He looks the part."

Aguirre doesn't seem convinced, but before he can reply the entire group of men turns toward them, starts clapping, and demands that Vergo speak, speak, speak. He pacifies the atmosphere with a show of his raised palms.

"Thank you. Thank you all," says Vergo. "You've done an extraordinary job."

More applause. Vergo raises his voice.

"At first, some of you were skeptical about the operation. I want to tell you that I understand that. Attacking other men, men like us, is what they did, what our enemies did, for months. But the context changes, and when the context changes the objectives change. We must show the world that women can't control themselves, that they're dangerous, and that's why we have to control them. Every woman has a sick hormone, a menstruation in her brain. They are manipulative uteruses. Those men you wounded weren't real men, just dogs. Lapdogs, submissive, seduced by a wrongheaded idea of the world, like slaves following their masters' orders. Today we have freed them. We have shown them the chains that bound them. Their blood will give them a reason to live, just as..."

One of the security guards interrupts Vergo. He whispers something in his ear and gestures for him to follow. The men are silent, confused.

Vergo looks through a window with wooden slats.

It's Ramos. Without his mask. Dressed as a woman. In the middle of the street.

Although it's not just Ramos: around him, at a distance of a few meters, are about a hundred Princesses, maybe more. FeConGuard cars with their siren lights on, blocking traffic. Police cordons. On the streets around the main avenue, a tide of women adjusting their masks approach the building. Farther on are the first cameras. There are no sounds heard, not even birdsong.

"From behind too!" shouts another guard.

The men react to his warning and try to see outside. The scene—so dramatic and unexpected—is terrifying: a man dressed as a woman surrounded by hundreds of women with a single face, at the ready, like a chorus about to begin a requiem, just waiting for the sign from the conductor.

Before fear can take hold inside the building, Vergo asks the men to remain calm, to stop pacing, and to keep quiet. He doesn't want distractions. He doesn't want anyone asking questions. He looks through the slats again. They are surrounded. And then he sees her.

She emerges from an army of motionless masks, like a floating body.

She stands beside Ramos.

Vergo holds his breath.

It's her.

Najwa looks toward the building. She is still wearing the same clothes she had on at the event in the park, a discreet dress, but she's taken off her high heels, and her stockings are torn. Then she looks at Ramos and circles him, studying his dress, his makeup, observing his painted nails, his brunette wig. She moves slowly, like a crocodile.

She stands behind him.

And with one swift motion she tears off his dress, revealing two enormous fake tits, tighty-whities sweat through between his butt cheeks, and two emaciated, flaccid hairy legs that tremble like dice in a shaker. Ramos falls to his knees and bursts into tears.

Najwa approaches one of the FeConGuard cars.

"We know what you've done," she says through the car's public address system. Her voice echoes between the nearby buildings. "We know you're in there. You're surrounded, with no way out. The government is aware of the situation and will inform the population over the next few hours. The FeConGuard is charged with your arrest and will turn you over to the justice system. We also know how many of you there are."

Inside the building, Hugo is absorbed in watching the screens, seeing how the hashtags change and how journalists offer breaking news reports. He confirms what Najwa is saying.

"How is it possible that we've been found out?" someone shouts.

"That bastard betrayed us! That son of a bitch, that punk-ass piece of shit! He betrayed us!"

"No! Ramos would never do that! He's one of us!"

Vergo shakes his head: Ramos is innocent. He has to be innocent. Najwa continues speaking.

"We don't want more violence. We don't want anyone else to get hurt. We've suffered enough damage today, all of us. So I demand that you come out peacefully, one by one, and hand yourselves over. None of the women with me will attack you, I promise. Their presence here is symbolic: we want to prove that we are the majority, and that society is with us. We want to prove that you are a memory of something that no longer works, that never worked, and that your actions are futile. You have five minutes. If you aren't out by then, the FeConGuard will be forced to enter."

All the men look at Vergo. Hugo keeps cursing Ramos's betrayal, and few still defend him. There is no consensus as to what they should do: some of them suggest turning themselves in and accepting their sentences; others want to try to escape via the roof; a small minority wants to stick it out, as long as it takes to find a way out of the building and back to their lives, as if nothing had ever happened.

"Do we have a megaphone, an amplifier, anything like that?" asks Vergo.

Hugo places a headset with a microphone onto his head and brings the computer equipment over to the window. Then he connects several loudspeakers to the computer.

Vergo speaks.

"You are all whores and bitches," he begins.

It had been a long time since Najwa had heard his voice, almost as long as it'd been since she'd seen him in person. She'd followed his trajectory through random images, online texts, videos that threatened them. Especially before the Truce, when the streets were aflame and Phallic State still had some power. He never revealed himself, but it was too easy for her to recognize him: the same clothes, that absurd bandanna over his nose like in a Western, his enormous, sad eyes, glancing downward. Absolutely ridiculous. She always sensed that he wanted her to find him out, and maybe that was why he didn't hide those tics, gestures, and arguments that gave him away.

She missed fucking him.

"We are heavily armed," he continues.

The men look at each other, and then at the floor, as if some piece of information had somehow gotten away from them.

"We aren't going to turn ourselves in. We are acting in the name of many men like us, who will never surrender. Your ideas seek to destroy the history that has brought us to where we are: social progress, workers' rights, art, stability, democracy. Who achieved all that? We did! Men! And where were you while we were killing ourselves to make the world a better place? Hiding at home. Safe and sound. Waiting for our blood to spill so you could cry over us, sure, but never on the front lines, never fighting for what mattered. And you know it, you know it as well as we do. Your cowardice is your identity and your punishment, bitches."

An uncomfortable ripple runs through the Princesses. A murmur of voices envelops Vergo's words. The first rocks fly through the air, hitting the building's facade with a weak thud. The FeConGuard tries to hold the perimeter, but the bodies are vibrating like a nest of ants. Vergo raises his voice, filling the street with his vocal cords.

"If we leave the building, all bets are off. We will come out ready to kill. Our hands will not tremble. And if you attack us, you'll make us into martyrs. The whole world will see what women do. The whole world will see the faces you hide behind your masks. So forget about it. Take your fucking panties and your cunt guard and get the fuck out. Go home, go back to ruining the lives of the poor schmucks who live with you. But don't tell us what we have to do, because, as always, you don't have a fucking clue."

The men around Vergo start losing their shit, sensing an eminent catastrophe. A group desperately rushes up the stairs, looking for somewhere to hide. Others argue among themselves. The rest, about fifty men, raise their fists. If they have to sacrifice themselves, they will. They will not abandon their leader. Aguirre is not among them.

Hugo, Bruno, and Donovan are. Vergo finishes his speech.

"You have thirty seconds to clear the street."

Najwa sees women jumping over the Fe-ConGuard's cordon. They are picking up rocks and sticks from the ground, and distributing tiny objects like nail files, keys, and pens.

"Twenty!"

Some of them are carrying their high-heeled shoes by the instep, with the stiletto point facing forward, like a sharp knife.

"Ten!"

She is unarmed. Ramos covers his head with his hands.

Intake of breath.

The door opens.

Exhale.

And the men come out half-dressed, some in colorful skirts, and stockings, most of them in T-shirts or bare-chested, with all sorts of objects in their hands, computer mice, clothes hangers, cell phones, beer cans, shrieking like animals escaped from the zoo, grunting without words, two by two, three by three, a stampede running toward a wall, leaving their cage, free at last, to destroy everything in their wake. The women receive them like a shield trying to stop a projectile sent from a catapult, absorbing them and vomiting them out, and then bouncing back at them, falling on them, burying them under a scrum of flesh, a tombstone that moves along the ground without releasing the still-living body beneath it.

It was them, thinks Najwa. They started it; they came at us.

Before coming through the door, Hugo, tears welling up in his eyes, looks at Vergo: he seems calm, after taking off the headphones he runs his hand through the bit of hair he has left, as if preparing for a date. Outside, men fall to the ground dramatically, screaming horribly, tasting defeat. Hugo's fear over what is happening is not assuaged by his leader, who suddenly, fleetingly, lets out a smile. It is not a proud smile, or a smug one, but a happy smile. A joyful one. A smile that lights up his eyes, hides his scar and softens it. He is a man seeing a sunset for the first time. A boy finishing a jigsaw puzzle or stomping an anthill. Hugo understands. He shudders. The ground opens up beneath his enormous boots.

"Vergo," he says, "Ramos was sold down the river from the beginning, right?"

"Yes."

"You gave the Princesses our location?"

"Yes."

"Can I ask you why, you goddamn flaming son of a bitch?"

Vergo looks at him with disgust, as if his question doesn't deserve an answer.

"You're pathetic," says Hugo.

Vergo laughs. "Like all of you."

Hugo insults him several more times, and then, unable to hold back his tears, the furious teenager he once was, and still is inside, leaves the building and gallops toward a jumbled mass of female bodies that awaits him impatiently, and he launches himself into them headfirst, like a billy goat trying to clear a forest, blindly, bellowing, not understanding that the forest has already overtaken everything.

Vergo is the last to emerge. He pulls an object out of his pocket, hides it in his sleeve, and crosses the threshold.

He walks so slowly that the women, who are focused on repelling and suffocating his predecessors, scarcely notice he is among them. He leaps on a mountain of tangled bodies, as if he didn't hear the screams, or they were insignificant, or he didn't want to be bothered. He is looking for Najwa.

He finds her.

And when he sees her he feels a very brief twinge of sadness, a strand of razor wire slicing him and bringing up uncomfortable questions: Where would he like to be now? With whom? For how long?

Don't look at her. Don't think. Don't respond.

She races toward him, still holding the car's microphone, and as she runs the cord is torn out of the dashboard, cracking it open. Four meters of plastic and copper follow her like a foreign appendage, invertebrate, tangling in her legs. She looks like a being from another world.

There are four meters separating them now.

Three meters.

Two.

One.

Hello, my love. Long time no see.

Najwa recognizes the man he was before the scar. Vergo slaps her brutally on the jaw, without a word, a slap so perfect it looks like well-rehearsed choreography, a performance, a simulation. And just as he reveals a knife in his right hand and lifts it, and waves it threateningly, just before turning it to hold it by the blade, Najwa and her Princesses stop him and push his tattooed arm toward his body, before that piece of metal slices through his flesh and his ribs and enters his heart, before he dies and becomes the last heir in a line of barbarians, the last reader of an ancient, crumbling book, before any and all of that, Vergo winks at her.

And she smiles back at him.

EPILOGUE

IMPROPER APPROPRIATION:

An Introduction to the Polemic[1]

Dr. Aixa de la Cruz, PhD

University of the Basque Country

Department of Anglo-American

Feminist and Gender Studies

August 2046

Only on extremely rare occasions does an academic publication achieve the massive repercussions that the volume edited by Claudia Vázquez and her colleagues at the Universidad Autónoma de Madrid's Department of Emancipation has over the last six months. A result, like this book, of a commission from the Ministry of Dignity, *La voz de las Princesas* (The voice of the Princesses)[2] commemorates the twenty-fifth anniversary of the Scorched Revolution with a collection of interviews and critical essays that would never have transcended the university realm if not for the surprising testimony of Najwa López de la Torre. The young researcher who broke the case showed up unannounced at the home of the spokesperson for the Princesses, with no expectation that she would get through the door.

Najwa López de la Torre had been out of the public eye for years. Not even the Minister of Dignity had managed to extend her a personal invitation to participate in the project. But as the doctoral student recalled with a laugh, "I was in her neighborhood, and figured what do I have to lose?"

She rang the bell and was met by López de la Torre herself, who had "just rolled out of bed, in a bathrobe, because she was expecting a package of books and thought I was the delivery person. I introduced myself as a student in the Teachers for Equality Training Program, and to make up for the misunderstanding she invited me in to have breakfast with her. We ate muesli with kefir." The rest is history.

I asked the researcher, who was Dr. Vázquez's intern, if López de la Torre explained her reasons for breaking twenty-five years of silence so spontaneously, and she said that López de la Torre was cryptic about her motives. However, as demonstrated in the transcription of their conversation, after a very bad coughing fit she admitted that she was suffering from Stage III metastatic cancer, which ended up killing her. She also made it clear that she was refusing chemotherapy "because it makes no sense to go against the wishes of your body, and if mine wants to multiply, I will comply with those wishes."[3] Indeed, the more than thirty-page interview published in *La voz de las Princesas* is the testimony of a woman who knows her death is imminent and wants to leave her affairs in order. This is seen in her numerous rectifications of mistakes made in her political career, in the attacks of Prime Minister Sánchez—particularly regarding her decision to rebaptize the former Ministry of Women's Rights as the less identity-based Ministry of Dignity—and in that final rousing speech addressed to future generations, warning them of the dangers of economic prosperity, "which makes our critical judgment grow lethargic and turns us into submissive slaves, the words *thank you* always on our lips for the charity the powerful give us."[4]

In short, it seems evident that López de la Torre decided to break her silence *then* due to her impending death, and that the young age of her interviewer may have been another incentive—she saw in her the incarnation of the generation to whom she wanted to address her final words. As I will try to demonstrate in the pages that follow, one could also infer the nature of the wariness that kept her silent for twenty-five years. Therefore, we can explain why she kept that information quiet, why she divulged it when she did, and even why she chose an intern as her confidante. But what will always be a mystery is simply and straightforwardly why, why speak and betray herself, or betray us? Judging by the political debate it has raised, the negative repercussions that her revelations could cause within the context of the feminist struggle and the fight for women's dignity are considerable, and I will devote a section of this article to outlining them, although readers can find a more exhaustive analysis of them in the articles by Katixa Agirre and Edurne Portela that follow. As an introduction to this pluralistic and multidisciplinary project with which we aspire to raise awareness within various social agents of the need to approach the I. R. R. case cautiously, I have taken the liberty of pointing out the essentials of the case, based on my personal experience as an academic before and after the Revolution, as an activist, a privileged witness to our more recent history, and as a woman.

THE ROUGH YEARS

I met López de la Torre when she was just Najwa; in fact, both of us were just first names on the lips of professors at the Universidad Complutense in Madrid, where I studied English language and literature and she studied history. We both attended meetings of the Feminist Student Collective that she ended up leading and that later became the first group of Princesses, the one that covered Madrid in the M/W flags and that began the movement. It was 2007, and feminist theory, formerly conceived as the only discipline in which women were the subject and object of knowledge, began to be incorporated into the more inclusive gender studies, which had emerged from the idea that "woman" and "man" were empty labels with no true meaning[5]—opening the field up to the interference of academics specializing in branches such as "new masculinities" and gay studies. We changed the signs on our departments, we opened up our offices to all the enemies of binary sexual identity, and we were both generous and stupid as we shared with men the only small oasis of academic power that our mothers had passed down to us.

When I received my doctorate in 2017, the worst predictions of the enemies of gender relativism had come to pass. By accepting a feminism without women, we had achieved a feminism filled with men. I competed against a man for, and lost to him, the first position I applied to at the Institute of Gender Studies of Granada. Dr. Gerardo Gómez entered as a full professor, based on a stay at Oxford and a thesis that, following in the footsteps of Eric Anderson,[6] took as its premise the belief that the essential trait of normative masculinity is homophobia, and that rooting it out would put an end to the whole issue. If this characteristic prejudice is overcome, the theory went, the quintessentially oppressive and oppressing gender would topple under its own weight. Gómez applied this premise to Spain, and maintained that, since the 2006 gay marriage law, our country had led the way toward a new egalitarian era that was beginning to materialize in the increasingly large number of men who defined themselves as gay-friendly. The mechanisms through which that new "homotolerant" masculinity was going to end the power imbalances between men and women were unclear, but were taken for granted, just as it was taken for granted that we were inexorably approaching an inclusive utopia that would lead us to the *new* man and the process of transformation he had undergone by force of will. Dr. Gómez's thesis was celebrated for its original focus, but the only difference between his postulates and those of his colleagues was marked by his naive optimism.[7]

When I was studying for my master's in gender, my class was made up of twenty-four women and two men. When I taught my first class in a similar program, the numbers had evened out, but not the balance of power. In a group of twenty-four students to whom I had explained the power differences created by gender stereotypes, ten men managed to get the debate to revolve around whether the original sin of being born an oppressor just for having a penis wasn't infinitely more difficult than settling into the comfortable role of victim, where compassion replaced guilt.

Outside of the academy, in the cybernetic universe that was López de la Torre's habitat, a similar scene was playing out. I remember the case documented by Luna Miguel in *Los años duros* (The Rough Years)[8] about the campaign sparked by the #MeToo hashtag that encouraged women to share on social media their experiences with sexual harassment and abuse in order to raise awareness of how widespread the problem is. Some activists pointed out that it wasn't fair that it always fell on women to expose themselves, and they encouraged the aggressors to take part in the initiative with acts of contrition. There were two types of responses. On one hand, there were men who accepted this mea culpa exercise: their posts were received with congratulations and praise for their courage and integrity, and were shared more than the testimonies of the victims. On the other hand, those who didn't want to take part in the campaign took armor-plated refuge in their absolute innocence, while at the same time harassing the activists, calling them in one case "feminazis who aren't real feminists, because they aren't trying to create equality, and only interested in accusing men of being the enemy, criminalizing us and fanning the flames of a war of the sexes that we thought was over."[9]

We were living in what I named the Mr. Hyde Era,[10] the dark flip side of postmodern relativism. On a geopolitical scale, we were suffering it with Donald Trump, the US president who popularized the concept of post-truth and who shielded himself behind the premise that single stories do not exist but rather that there are multiple versions of each fact, as a way of invalidating reliable media sources; contemporary art had fallen into the conceptual meaninglessness of the old vanguards, and public universities were holding conferences on feminism without a single female speaker. Perhaps influenced by my Hegelian education, I refused to accept, in the theoretical realm, that the way out of that well of sophisms implied a return to our roots, to essentialist feminism—although that was what happened in the thirties with the arrival of the biologism of Cyclical Feminism.[11] I prayed for someone more utopian than me, capable of believing in pure, stable categories, who would provoke social activism in the streets. And then Najwa came along, someone who never subscribed to that idea that "woman" was an arbitrary label incapable of defining a homogenous collective. As she explained at the Second Conference on the Politics of Sisterhood, women existed "not because of their genitalia, or their reproductive function, or the performative gestures they enact," but rather because of "the oppression they've been victims of,"[12] and only by uniting around that oppression can they put an end to the power imbalances that, as I have illustrated, are reproduced even among academics who have declared the death of sexual difference.

THE '21 REVOLUTION AND ITS CONTEXT

The Princess movement created a sense of community among Spanish women by invoking symbols associated with femaleness: blood-red graffiti, Disney characters, bonfires of high-heeled shoes... According to the evolutionary fallacy, the actions they undertook and the ideology underpinning them should have been stripped of their weight because they weren't *innovative*, they were reminiscent of May '68, and ours was a different world, individualistic, reluctant to be thrown into the same basket. However, there were the hosts of activists renouncing their *I* in favor of *we*, hiding behind masks to blend into a crowd that revealed only the face of gendered oppression and that, I told myself, marked the end of an era. The success of the movement lay in the idea that a minimum common denominator can always be established, because there are universal, binding ties that transcend class, race, and sexual orientation. The '21 Revolution diluted the peripheral independentist movements, but remains very linked to their rise, because the Princesses, like so many nations throughout history, grew stronger in the face of a clear enemy, and it was that enemy that defined them. López de la Torre understood that "women" were those whom the patriarchy oppressed without that oppression being countered by solid privileges—unlike "men," who, no matter how much they were repressed by certain expectations inherent in their masculine role, always came out ahead[13]—but she was not the leader of women but of the Princesses, who defined themselves as "subjects susceptible to being victims of violence by Phallic State." Theirs was a very inclusive movement, because, paradoxically, so was those terrorists' hatred.

The interpretation of the Revolution of '21 as one caused by external provocation has always existed. However, until López de la Torre's posthumous testimony was published, divergent readings were possible. In fact, the most widely accepted reading suggested that if the Princesses were a response to Phallic State, it was, in turn, the reaction of a group of men to the gradual loss of privileges inherent in the policies of equality. The loop of action–reaction did not have a locatable source that would allow our recent history to be read like one of those movies from the 1960s, where the heroine turns into a vigilante after and only after being humiliated by a band of rapists. The theory of external male agency was one among many, and because it was the only one that injured the self-esteem and transgressive potential of the Princesses, it was easy, as well as convenient, to rule it out. However, as several of the articles in this very volume make clear, it is now the most popular position.

APPROPRIATION OF THE CAUSE: I. R. R.'S MASTER PLAN

Vergo. We only knew his alias, and after he was executed, the government refused to release his real name to avoid pilgrimages to his grave by nostalgics, or any sort of media recognition. All we were left with were his initials, and we soon forgot them. I. R. R. A shadow of the past that we didn't want to darken the new Feminist Republic we had won for ourselves and future generations. Najwa López de la Torre served two terms as the head of the Ministry of Emancipation, the transitional department that preceded the also-extinct Ministry of Women's Rights, and when she finished her second term in office she distanced herself from politics. It seemed that she didn't want to cloud the postrevolutionary springtime with the specters of her combat experience. She was barely thirty-seven, but she was already old for the world she had helped to build. She accepted a post at the Universidad Autónoma de Madrid and taught "A History of the Struggle" to several generations of students, until she asked for a leave of absence in 2040 and disappeared. During her final years, she received and rejected endless institutional invitations, tributes, and interview requests. She chose discretion, and that has made it very difficult to reconstruct who she was. Recently, various media outlets have tried to investigate her personal life by harassing those close to her, using paparazzi tactics they seem to have thought better of, thankfully. The magnates of the large media groups offered their kingdoms for an exclusive from her mother, for the name of a lover or friend, but López de la Torre surrounded herself with a small core group of people who were as tight-lipped as she was. Fortunately, they are keeping the flames from spreading beyond the political debate surrounding the *official account* (another retrograde concept that is making a comeback, like biological essentialism).

How does this missing piece revealed by López de la Torre's testimony affect the historical account? What is implied in her ex-boyfriend, the founder of Phallic State, supposedly sacrificing himself for our cause? I would like to answer that question by reviewing the opinions declared by the main Spanish press outlets about the case. The day the scandal broke, the digital newspaper *Nuevos Tiempos* titled their editorial "I. R. R.: The Gospel According to Judas." Antonio Marías Arévalo compared "the hidden face of the Princess Revolution" with the apocryphal Gospel, of dubious authenticity, that the National Geographic Society restored and translated in 2006. It offered a positive reading of the Apostle Judas Iscariot, suggesting that he handed Jesus over to the Romans according to a plan previously drawn up by his master. "In order to fulfill his destiny as a redeemer, the prophet needed an inglorious martyr. Many would have died for him, but only the most faithful of his disciples would have accepted the eternal flagellation reserved for traitors, a sacrifice devoid of glory, an act of absolute heroism." He wasn't the only one who gleaned biblical overtones in "the *true* [emphasis mine] story" of Vergo the terrorist.[14] Corpress, the journalistic text analysis software, reveals that, since the case was exposed, the press has acknowledged a more than 200 percent increase in the reference corpus (compiled between 2002 and 2045) in lexemes related to Christian mythology.[15] In one of the more recent examples, I. R. R. makes the shift from Judas to Christ. In a feature story published in *Nuevos Tiempos*, María José de Tomás compared the government's reluctance to include I. R. R. in the Museum of the Revolution with "the folly of those atheists who deny the existence of Jesus of Nazareth, as if his historical figure did not exist independently of the myth constructed around him."[16] The parliamentary initiative proposed by the mixed group did not demand that I. R. R.'s name lead the plaque of heroes on the museum facade, but if defenders of his inclusion are comparing him to the Christian redeemer, it is not hard to imagine the symbolic canvas being painted in their heads. In the *Last Supper* they've been dreaming up since February 2nd, Najwa López de la Torre, Marisa Suárez, Belén Mariscal, Ainhoa Zúñiga, and the other visible faces of the movement crowd around the messiah.

The conservative media's interest in vindicating the character described by López de la Torre is the more or less conscious manifestation of their anxiousness to reinstate a man at the center of our national myth. The Princesses led a process of change that mitigated territorial disputes, and the political parties of the '78 regime know they are indebted to them. This territorial integrity safeguarded by the feminist project shields it from challenges by centrist and right-wing factions, but that doesn't keep their representatives and constituents from feeling excluded by the symbology that brings us together.

Hence their interest in recovering the figure of a heroic I. R. R., because it allows them to insert into the Second Transition the elements of male authority and agency (so present in the first Transition), thus uniting the old and the new, the lost and the gained.

If I am correct, readers may be wondering what's wrong with granting them this small concession, and here emerges a debate that is already being discussed by feminist theorists. An introduction to it can be found in this book's essay by Nere Basabe. She endorses "a small symbolic defeat to ensure a project that will only achieve its maximum potential when consolidated by consensus." Although I admit to the merit, on a pragmatic level, of her position, we cannot forget the importance the symbolic has always held in the fight against the patriarchy, nor can we minimize the implications that arise within the collective imagination when suggesting that female emancipation was the result of a man's master plan. According to López de la Torre, I. R. R. himself was aware, albeit not initially, of the significance of his interference: "He realized that he was guilty of absolute mansplaining, assuming he had the right to push us into action as if we didn't know what was best for us, and that was when he decided to sacrifice himself."[17] Provoking the feminist protestors into eliminating him in self-defense was a new act of imposition, but if, as he *supposedly* wanted, the intention hidden behind his actions was not revealed, Vergo would have managed to escape the trap his male subjectivity had led him into.

The history of man as subject is a story of illicit appropriations, and I. R. R. sums it up with unique weight. Just like many of the male theorists who were drawn to gender studies, he couldn't be both the object and subject of the knowledge he usurped from women. He discovered the feminist cause and studied it in order to lead it, dominate it, to change it, instead of changing himself and other men. He believed that a bunch of readings and a series of conversations with his girlfriend freed him from the inertias of his role, from the arrogance of someone born into a world made for and by those of his stock, and he was unable to escape his perspective to see what he was doing—moving marionette strings as if he were an omnipotent god—because his identity was always *the* identity, his status *the* norm, and someone who believes himself to be universal isn't looking from the margins. The fact that I reject the official recognition of I. R. R.'s role, because I reject our recent past being written as history has always been written—with active men and reactive women, with redeemers who sacrifice themselves for our souls—does not imply that I do not understand his tragedy, as ancient as that of Oedipus Rex (who only lost his eyes, while I. R. R. lost his head). I. R. R. succumbed to the biases imposed on him by a culture that always precedes the individual, and he died in order to escape said biases. What I struggle to understand, as I hinted at earlier, is the decision made by López de la Torre, who kept silent for twenty-five years precisely because she sensed the ideological implications that would result from her divulging this secret. She always knew what it would entail or, at the very least, since her college days when she read Carol Clover[18] and wrote the following critique of the film *Mad Max: Fury Road* (2015), now held in the digital archive of the Universidad Complutense and publicly available, in which she laments that

> one of the few action films written with a feminist agenda [. . .] falls into the trap of depicting a group of women who tolerate the imbalances of power they are relegated to by their gender within the established patriarchal order until a man attacks them and they take up arms only after this direct aggression. [. . .] Is it so hard to imagine a world in which our agency is not the result of male provocation?[19]

I. R. R. acted out of blindness, but López de la Torre devoted her academic life to the study of gender representations. She distanced herself from politics and focused on the university because she knew that the only way to change the deep structures of the patriarchy was through educating future generations, through teaching them *to see* that which I. R. R. had never seen. What happened inside her head during those final days, sick and alone, shouldn't obscure the decades of service she gave us. In fact, I fear a future in which the history books erase her with a secondary designation, "the girlfriend of," or "the muse who inspired," because said future will force us to read her death as a self-sacrifice. The Najwa/Vergo binary will be an inversion of opposites: the man who died for women versus the women who've died for men throughout history. And if post-structuralism has bequeathed us anything positive, it is that binaries shouldn't be inverted. They should be deconstructed, dynamited at their very root.

NOTES

1 This article originally appeared in *Relecturas de un pasado reciente*, edited and with an introduction by Elisabeth Falomir, 2047.

2 Claudia Vázquez et al., *La voz de las Princesas: 25 años sin muro* (Madrid: Ministry of Dignity, 2045).

3 Quoted in Vázquez, 79.

4 Quoted in Vázquez, 87.

5 In *Gender Trouble* (New York: Routledge, 1990), Judith Butler dismantles the gender/sex binary. The theorists

who preceded her assumed that sex was natural, and gender a construction, but she maintains that sex is also discursive, because the ideology precedes the subject, so there is no way to read sexual difference *before* culture. Imagine a planet called Dactylia that is known for its veneration of classical music and where social groups are identified by their hands. There are the "pianists," with long, thin fingers, and the "jai alai players," with thick, calloused hands. The pianists are educated according to a series of rules and with a series of privileges (e.g., it is understood that they are genetically gifted for music and fill the conservatories, which are the planet's main centers of political and intellectual power) that the jai alai players do not have. The "hands" dimension on Dactylia would be like the "sex" dimension on Earth. The Dactylians maintain that assigning one label or another (pianists/jai alai players) is not arbitrary, but rather "comes with their bodies." However, that anatomical difference is only read as an essential difference in the cultural realm.

In our culture, no one would be categorized based on their fingers, and so no one would understand how one's hands could be as determinant as one's sex. Butler's controversial and often-misinterpreted statement that biological sex does not exist must be understood in those terms, as should her rejection of the concept of "sexual identity." When we deconstruct the sex/gender opposition, we also dynamite the oppositions of man/woman, feminine/masculine, heterosexual/homosexual, etc. In the binary conception, one is born "girl" or "boy" and then adopts one of the two genders associated with each sex, "feminine" or "masculine," which in turn are considered predisposed toward a certain sexual inclination.

But if there are not two sexes, the binary system that unfolds based on that dichotomy falls apart. Faced with exclusive labels, Butler opts for the proliferation of difference. "Woman," like any collective, excludes marginal members who do not fit within its central definition. Naming means establishing borders, selecting the most characteristic features, and excluding the examples that depart from the broad definition encapsulated within the category. For Butler, the problem with feminism is that it has chosen "woman" as its object, and "woman" has no meaning; it is certainly not universal. Egalitarian feminism of the sixties and seventies that advocated sisterhood between all the world's women based on a shared history of oppression often made the mistake of speaking for white heterosexual women, denying the problems particular to lesbian, transsexual, and racialized bodies, etc. As the author explains in *Gender Trouble*, the feminist insistence on the "coherence and unity of the category of women has effectively refused the multiplicity of cultural, social, and political intersections in which the concrete array of "women" are constructed" (19–20).

6   Eric Anderson, *Inclusive Masculinity: The Changing Nature of Masculinities* (New York: Routledge, 2009).

7   Despite her manifest rejection of the emergence of masculinity studies in the late nineties, Tania Modleski, in *Feminism Without Women* (New York: Routledge, 1991), conceded that there was a path the incipient discipline could take that would ally it *with* feminism and not *against* it. She described it as an analysis of "male power, male hegemony, with a concern for the effects of this power on the female subject," an analysis that is always alert, aware that men tend to appropriate "femininity" while oppressing women (6–7). We could define that latter path, according to Modleski, as the enemy path— one that approached feminist theory in order to loot its tools for the study of men, by men and for men, in order to conclude that they too are historical victims of an imposed gender, to liken their oppression to ours and avoid any critical examination of their privileges—and declare, not without some sadness, that that was the one

that took hold in Spanish academia in the early 2020s and didn't lose steam until well into the postrevolutionary transitional phase.

8 Luna Miguel, *Los años duros* (Barcelona: Círculo de Tiza, 2023).

9 Comment left on Luna Miguel's Facebook page, 2018, quoted in *Los años duros*, 37. Translation mine.

10 Aixa De la Cruz, *Dr. Jekyll y Mr. Hyde: la deriva del pensamiento posmoderno* (Madrid: Niebla Editorial, 2040).

11 The term "Cyclical Movement" appeared for the first time in the September 2034 issue of *Todxs juntxs*, which, in a wink to the essentialist turnaround that it put forth, had an image of the female reproductive system on the cover and spelled the magazine's title in the prerevolutionary way: *Todas juntas.* Among the invited authors were Jordan Novales, Barbara Ferris, and Fernanda Núñez, all three from the world of medicine and biology. Since the seventies, no feminist trend had been based on the biological determinism proposed by the cyclical feminists. In fact, modern feminism had traveled quite directly along a continuum between one pole (identity-based positions) and the other (difference-based ones), but it had never departed from the more basic notion of "gender" as a cultural construct motivated by social factors rather than physiological ones. To find precedents for a hermeneutics similar to the one proposed by the cyclical feminists, we would have to go back to the paleoanthropological perspective popular in the sixties, which located the origin of gender differences in the paleolithic era, when the population was divided into hunters and gatherers, and women took on the latter role because of their anatomy. That correlation between sexual dimorphism and gender attitudes had remained abandoned by academia until the cyclical feminists proclaimed their particular "return to the body." They were searching for a theory that could integrate the various models from French post-structuralism to postmodern

relativism, and that was bolstered by rigorous physio-logical models. Although they reacted against Butler by insisting that "sex matters" and by returning to a binary system of sexual identification, they shared the primary concerns of the author of *Gender Trouble* and reinterpreted them without entirely refuting them. The Cyclical Movement defends the existence of a discreet category of "woman" but splits feminine subjectivity into different phases or cycles that seek to include dif-ference (such as intersex and transgender people), and accept that gender is a discourse that precedes sexual differentiation and is not a *natural* reading of physiolog-ical changes—"bodily fluids do not have language"—but rather a misinterpretation of them, imposed and perpet-uated by the dominant group. The following quote from Barbara Ferris's 2032 work *Woman Is Bleeding* (12–13) clarifies the primary postulates of the movement:

> *"Woman" is a flexible identity that travels and can dock at various ports, which correspond to differ-ent physiological states. This includes the woman who does not yet bleed, the woman who bleeds, the woman who temporarily ceases to bleed, the woman who no longer bleeds, and the one who will never bleed, who is always in a state of "not yet." The woman who does not yet bleed is the one who receives the full weight of the culture, the discourse with which she will have to interpret the changes to come, in other words, her gender. A schoolyard where we distinguish boys from girls not because of their bodies, which cannot be sexed, but by their clothes, their haircuts, and their symbolic use of space shows that gender roles are learned before the emergence of the secondary sex characteristics that differentiate us, and with the objective of setting an asymmetrical and normative reading of said differ-ences. But the differences exist, as materialization and as hovering promise. The woman in her fertile period*

*who goes through the four phases of her menstrual cycle
is, in each of them, aware of the transitoriness of her
state, as the transsexual woman is, during or after her
transition, as is the prepubescent girl seeing herself in
her mother—whether or not she shares chromosomal
characteristics, which includes intersex people who were
raised as women—and as the mother who sees herself
in her grandmother, who no longer bleeds for different
reasons than gestating women, who will bleed again, or
presume that they will. It is that eternally being on the
precipice of change that is the basis of female identity,
who has been pathologized and medicalized by a culture
that defines the norm in terms of stability and coherence. As Erika Irusta said, we aren't crazy, we are
cyclical. Insanity is the terrain of the woman who does
not know or understand herself, the woman who denies
herself because she denies the radical difference of her
corporeal experience, and feminist action cannot, must
not, deny her as well. Our survival entails a reinven-
tion of the discourses that construct our stationary
identity and an activism designed to bring down the
institutions that demand a mutilation of our very nature
in order to have a place at the table. The systems of
capitalist production, the pharmaceutical companies that
design synthetic hormones, and the gynecologists who
medicate us from adolescence to camouflage the signs of
a body aching from the systemic abuse it is subjected to
are the primary enemies we are facing.*

12 *Actas del II Congreso de Políticas de Hermandad* (Madrid:
Museo de la Revolución, 2025), 25.

13 Najwa López de la Torre, *Conferencias en la Complutense*
(Madrid: Universidad Complutense de Madrid).

14 Antonio Marías Arévalo, "I. R. R.: El Evangelio según
Judas," *Nuevos Tiempos*, February 2, 2046.

15 Corpress Data, http://corpress.search.es, Accessed August 23, 2046.

16 María José De Tomás, "Cuando la ideología impugna la verdad histórica," *Nuevos Tiempos*, February 10, 2046.

17 Quoted in Vázquez, 89.

18 Carol Clover, *Men, Women and Chainsaws: Gender in the Modern Horror Film* (New York: Princeton University Press, 1992).

19 Najwa López de la Torre, "*Mad Max* y la infinita paciencia femenina," online archive of the Universidad Complutense de Madrid, 2017, accessed July 23, 2046.

ACKNOWLEDGMENTS

In order to write this book I copied fragments of private conversations and took advantage of theoretical knowledge that isn't part of my CV, but is part of the CVs of women near me. I was slow to ask for permission, to research and devote myself to essential reading, because *what the hell*, one of the women would sum it up for me. I laid down the gauntlet and launched into fiery speeches, trusting that my provocation would stimulate them. Et cetera. I think you get the idea.

The intellectual coauthors of this book have names. First of all, Aixa de la Cruz, who encouraged me to write it, warned me of its inherent ethical contradictions, and gave me enough space to realize them. As if that weren't enough, she also wrote this book's extraordinary epilogue. In addition to Aixa, on this list I include my mother, Nieves Ruiz; my sister, Adriana Repila; and my friends Adriana Coll and Nere Basabe (who came up with the concept of *manattributing*, for example). I wrung them all out over long hours, always assuming that they would be *thrilled* to respond.

Outside of that intimate circle, there are other women from whom I've taken materials that I can't name, because their Twitter threads that inspired me are buried in the depths of my timeline, and by the time I was writing this text their commentaries were already part of the popular domain of cyberspace. I can recognize in particular the coauthorship of Luna Miguel and María Sánchez—they are not my friends and I know them only from social media, but their reflections and debates helped me to explore territories that I hadn't considered, the contributions of women that they retweeted or mentioned, and the authors of numerous articles published in *Pikara* and *Playground*.

Last, the women I've been reading in recent years are also coauthors of this book. These creators have written fundamental books that situated me in a world adjusted to *true* reality, not the reality in which I considered myself a happy feminist from Monday to Friday, without commitment. I also include those women who, with their work and their lives, sometimes to the bitter end, managed to get those books written. Names like Rebecca Solnit, Nuria Varela, Kate Millett, Andrea Dworkin, Silvia Federici, and Jessa Crispin dialogue in my memory with others—María Moliner, Clara Campoamor, Virginia Woolf, Emilia Pardo Bazán, and Mary Wollstonecraft, to mention a few.

The final manuscript of this book was finished before the Weinstein scandal, #MeToo, the demonstrations on March 8, 2018, and #HermanaYoSíTe-Creo. If any of that can be recognized in these pages, it's only because the feminist movement has been waging a war for decades, a war that—on the one side—constantly repeats the same patterns of violence, humiliation, persecution, and terror, and on the other, the same strategies of solidarity, support, respect, and honesty.

Because yes, I believe that, as the hashtag made viral by Irantzu Varela declares, this is a war. One of the many we haven't wanted to acknowledge, by the way.

Finally, I would like to take advantage of these lines to thank Elvira Navarro, Katixa Agirre, Jon Bilbao, Santiago Pérez Isasi, Alejandro Morellón, and Elena Ramírez for their notes and comments on the first version of this book. I feel lucky and privileged to have been privy to all of their ideas.

IVÁN REPILA worked in advertising, graphic design, and publishing before turning to writing with his highly acclaimed debut novel, *Despicable Comedy*. His second novel, *The Boy Who Stole Attila's Horse*, was his first to appear in English. Repila's work is celebrated in his homeland of Spain and praised for its originality and depth, and has been translated into more than fifteen languages.

AIXA DE LA CRUZ is a Spanish writer of Basque origin. Her novel *Cambiar de idea* won the Premio Euskadi de Literatura and the Librotea Prize in 2020. In 2013 she was selected by the Spanish magazine *El Cultural* as one of twelve writers under 40 worth watching. In 2014 de la Cruz won the Cosecha Eñe, the annual prize for short stories from *Eñe* magazine. Her latest novel is *Las herederas* (Alfaguara, 2022).

MARA FAYE LETHEM is an award-winning translator of contemporary Catalan and Spanish prose, and the author of *A Person's a Person, No Matter How Small*. Her recent translations include books by Patricio Pron, Max Besora, Javier Calvo, Marta Orriols, Toni Sala, Alicia Kopf, and Irene Solà. She is currently translating the collected short stories of Pere Calders.